The Vigilante Chronicles

Warren Dent

ISBN 978-0-9978175-4-6

Printed in the United States of America

Acknowledgments

My writing group has been a constant source of review and critique on the stories contained in this collection. I thank the members for their insistence on 'showing', not 'telling' wherever possible, and on using dialog to present information that might otherwise sound like an entry in an encyclopedia.

Since some of the stories here are set in Australia and England, I've often used British spelling for select words. Please forgive me, as my reviewers have done.

Thanks to all.

Author's Note

There are eight stories here. Two set in London in 2012 are based on true public incidents that took place there. At the time they both made me extremely angry due to the lack of provocation, and that led to thoughts of wishful responses.

Two stories are set in Canada, specifically on Vancouver Island, British Columbia. In one, there is slight carryover into the U.S. Both these stories, as presented, represent incidents that have taken place in various countries across the world.

Many folks think that lawful responses to the types of violent events presented are not tough enough or severe enough. Which leads to the instigation of vigilante deeds where distraught people take the law into their own hands.

In 1825, 35 years after the first convicts were transported from Britain to the antipodes, Sydney was still a rough town. Lawlessness was rampant in some of the less salubrious areas where emancipists and convicts lived side by side. The four stories from that town in this book are based on recorded incidents but do not reflect any specific cases. They take place in locations that are true to the times.

Dedication

To all the men and women in security forces who seek and apprehend criminals. I applaud their ability to maintain control and exercise humane treatment when confronting purveyors of atrocious actions against humankind.

I doubt I could do what they do.

The Vigilante Chronicles

Warren Dent

Table of Locations used in Stories

Sydney, Australia, 1825

Table of Contents

High Boots

Mick rolls onto his side to relieve the cramp in his back. Dust left by a thousand boots rises from the floor and fills his nostrils. He snorts the dust out and swipes one of his shirt sleeves under the base of his nose. "Strewth, the crap a man puts up with!" he exclaims to himself. "Dirt, dirt everywhere. Dust in the pub, mud in the street, and soot in the chimneys. Wonder when they'll make nice tar roads like we 'ad back in Liverpool. Ah, strewth. Can't stand this, I'll just go peek out the winda."

He stands well back in the dark room, itches his crotch and stretches his arm towards the ceiling. If he jumped he could touch one of the beautiful old hardwood logs put in place in 1800, 25 years before. The pub's proprietor, Rob Bundy, is proud of the pub he and his cousins built back then, using timber they cut up-country themselves. Blackbutt eucalyptus, found twenty miles north of Sydney, carted to The Rocks area by bullock drays, and cut into shape at the now defunct Dawes mill.

Mick has heard Rob's story many times, as well as how the pub got its name – Black & Blue – in recognition of the work it took to make it real. So much had changed in all the years gone by.

More and more convict ships are now emptying their holds full of criminals at the Quay, Darling Harbour has become the centre for booming overseas trade, and The Rocks home for hundreds of lower class city workers, visiting sailors, and unfortunately, some of the more hardened escaped convicts. Numerous dives serve as pubs and brothels. It is a tough, almost lawless spot.

Police rarely enter its narrow streets except when summoned to remove a dead body. The cops are mostly Irishmen, intensely disliked, considered as useless, and as bigoted as some of the convicts. Of course most had been convicts when they arrived and had by now served out their years of punishment. Mick hates all of them, the scar across his right cheek provided by a cop in a brawl between four policemen and a band of foreign sailors Mick had joined to help. He'd cut the back of that cop's leg pretty severely, even after the slashing that had been delivered to his cheek, but he still hoped to face the bastard again on his own some time.

Once in a while, especially in very cold weather, his jaw aches where the scar ends. It adds to his craggy looks in a way, and a thin copper coloured beard covers some of the wound closer to his ear. He has startling blue eyes and a full head of hair matching his beard in colour. Women are attracted to the ruggedness and strength he exudes. He boasts of many conquests as a result.

A moving light outside the grimy window brings him back to the present. Only a man with a lady of the night holding a small lamp out in front to light their progress. Mick stands stock still while they pass, then retreats to the back room and sits on the only chair there. Five minutes after three am. Perhaps it will be another wasted night. The two previous robberies had always been on a Friday night since that was the day all the lads got paid and spent their earnings in liquid fire.

A month has passed since the last burglar, and Mick has stayed in four different pubs since then. Who was to say the robber would strike again tonight? Even if he were to do so, which pub would be his target?

Mick and Drake had talked over the best way to apprehend the culprit. They agreed that the chap was certainly going after the bigger pubs. More loot of course for the same amount of work. Should they place someone in each of the big pubs, so they'd be sure to get their man, no matter where he turned up? That would mean cash out of their pockets for one thing. Plus they worried whether the chaps they hired would have the same motivation as themselves. Would those hired stay awake all night silently waiting? And if the robber turned up would they have the desire and ability to capture him? How well could they fight, or for that matter how fast could they run to catch the robber if he streaked away?

Most importantly of all, Mick and Drake had a reputation to uphold. If a robber grabbed a haul and got away in the presence of someone they hired, it would reflect badly on the trust that merchants had in them. Nope, the only people they could trust were themselves. And so they took turns each Friday night waiting inside the pub after the doors closed at midnight and the publican took himself upstairs to bed.

Time passes slowly and Mick reminisces about the petty crimes he had committed as a strapping 20 year old member of the Liverpool gang, 'The Swingers.' He'd worked his way up over five years to be number two in the organization. He was held in high regard by the members, although it was the leader who failed to stand up for him when the authorities finally caught him out. He'd been the sacrificial lamb for the gang's bad work that night. Served three years at His Majesty's pleasure in Middlesex jail before being transported to Sydney for the remaining four years of his sentence. The only thing good he'd done for himself in his period of incarceration was exercise, exercise, exercise.

Today, his arm, leg and neck muscles bulge almost obscenely. While a few inches shorter than Drake, he is the stronger of the two, as their frequent contests at arm wrestling attest. Patrons of the pubs loved watching the incredible struggles, which Mick always won. Taking money from strangers who thought they could beat either man was a popular pastime. Both had learned well just how much to fake and give before pinning an opponent's wrist to the tabletop.

Mick flexes his right bicep and burps as he shows the huge mound of flesh to an imaginary audience. He's about to do it again with the other arm when he hears a slight scraping sound.

His senses go to full alert, he cocks his head to the side and listens intently, trying to identify what he heard. There it is again. No, not scraping, rather cutting. Cutting? Sort of. Cutting and scraping both. Then it registers. The front door has two small decorative windows in it. The robber outside is cutting and scraping the putty that holds one of the windows in place. In the previous robberies everyone assumed the perpetrator had used some sort of universal key, as there were no signs of any forced entry.

In order to avoid a similar fate, Bundy, the publican at this pub, developed a more complex entry arrangement. Two different keys unlocked deadbolts, but one bolt could be drawn back only if opened simultaneously while lifting and rotating the iron door handle in a specific direction. It took a certain dexterity to manage. Few mastered it. The robber outside clearly knew the setup, for his approach circumvented the maneuvering of the handle. He planned to simply reach through the hole he was making, and lift the internal latch directly while inserting a key with the other hand. He would undo the other deadbolt beforehand.

Mick smirks. Cunning bastard this robber is for sure. But as Mick thinks further, something doesn't add up. The guy would have to have incredibly long arms to reach through and down to the latch while releasing the other bolt at the same time. Nope, couldn't be done...unless...unless there were two of them. Yes that was the only way.   If true it changed the game considerably.

Two robbers, not one. Mick thinks fast. Will they both come in or will one stay out and keep watch for passersby? Damn. He hopes they both come inside, otherwise the chap outside could easily run away while Mick deals with the one who comes in. He waits impatiently, fingering the black cosh stuck in his belt. He's done a lot of damage with this, his favourite weapon. Small, easy to grip and swing, attached to his wrist with a leather strap, shaped by a local craftsman to his own design copying from memory the one he used frequently in Liverpool. It can strike a near lethal blow to a forehead or temple as he well knows, and can definitely mangle and destroy an ear.

One by one, he noiselessly moves three stools from immediately in front of the bar to the back room. With two intruders he realizes he may need two weapons, so on his third trip he brings forth the heavy metal crowbar that he's had the blacksmith cut back to four feet in length. Carefully he lays it on the floor where the chairs were. It's hard to see in the shadow of the overhang of the massive natural one-piece wood bar.

He looks toward the entrance and sees the robbers have detached the window on three sides. They'll prise it loose in just a few seconds so he scurries into the recesses of the back room to wait.

The pair outside struggle a little bit coordinating their efforts with the deadbolt and latch. Mick hears one of them swear, and the second man grunt in frustration. Two minutes later they succeed and gently push the door open. They pause, waiting to hear any reaction from within, then open the door further just sufficient to allow them entry. They move quickly, allowing Mick a very limited view of their shapes. Two thin guys, one much shorter than the other. They stop, allowing their eyes to adjust to the darkness, the only light coming from the tiny windows in the door. A crescent moon hardly helps.

Mick pulls his scarf up over his chin and mouth and tugs the black balaclava down over his forehead, so only his eyes and nose show. He's glad both men are in and the door closed. The taller chap saunters behind the bar and heads directly for the cash drawer. He's obviously been in the place before. He lifts the drawer carefully onto the counter, and grabs a handful of coins and notes. He passes them across the bar to his accomplice who deposits them in a large canvas bag. Mick wants them caught in the actual act. In transferring the second handful they've more than met that goal.

Mick springs forward, yelling ferociously at the top of his lungs "You bastards." In three strides he's behind the chap with the bag and wields his trusty cosh. Although shocked and surprised, the bagman starts to move to the side and Mick's cosh misses Its mark. Instead of a blow to the head the short truncheon lands on the chap's collarbone, the force cracking it instantly. The man grunts in pain, and the bag falls from his hands. He leans forward, his right arm crossing his chest so the hand can check the left shoulder. Mick lets his fury take hold and smashes the cosh hard up between the chap's legs. Doubling over, the man spits vomit down his trouser legs. Mick finishes him off with a punch to the chin, sending his victim out cold to the floor. The chap behind the counter is stunned by Mick's fury and runs for the door, pushing over chairs and tables in his way. Just as he reaches for the latch Mick thrusts out a leg and trips him.

The chap's head slams against the door and he falls to a sitting position. Mick retrieves the crow bar from its hiding place and advances, yelling, "Got you, you scum. Now you will pay." He and Drake have discussed what to do with victims. They know it's useless to simply hold them and turn them over to the cops. The thieves would simply buy their way to freedom from the corrupt Irish contingent and continue their ways, albeit most likely in a different area. Nope, what's appropriate is to make sure the perpetrators cannot continue their wayward habits. Neither vigilante is in to killing, although they've both done their share back home on distant shores. But maiming is something else and quite acceptable.

Mick debates what to do with the chap he now straddles on the floor. The victim is whining, pleading for mercy, looking more pathetic with every utterance. Mick's knee is crunching the man's balls and he holds the crowbar across the exposed Adam's apple, although not sufficient yet to cut off the whimpering and choking sounds. The bagman has shaken off the blow to his chin and is staring at Mick with eyes filled with hate. He snarls as he rises to a crouch, and produces a dagger from his boot. "There's two of us you maggot. You won't survive."

Mick's anger is at a fever pitch. He doesn't react immediately, but silently prepares for action. These scum would take a man's honest living away without a second thought. They deserve a beating.

Slowly Mick moves his left hand down the shaft of the crowbar, unseen by the bagman. As soon as that hand comes in contact with his right hand, Mick leans backwards, lifting the bar off the cashman's throat and swings it hard, smacking the bagman's ear and head with incredible force. Blood spurts from the ear and the three inch cut along the hairline. Mick jumps to his feet and kicks the bagman in the groin, asking, "You and what f...ing army will get me you shit?" As blood trickles from the chap's wounds Mick grabs the bagman's right hand and bends back the thumb and fingers breaking them one by one in succession.

He turns to find the cashman lifting the door latch, about to flee. Once again Mick swings the hefty crowbar and strikes the chap across the kidney on his left side. A follow-up swing breaks nearby bone, and his victim falls to the floor once again. As a coup de grace Mick breaks the chap's right hand fingers and thumbs, as done to his partner. It's very doubtful the pair will do any more grabbing of coins for a long time.

Mick knows that if he thinks about the violence and the damage done he will probably be a little regretful, so he makes himself busy picking up spilled coins he can see off the floor and putting them back in the drawer, placing the canvas bag with its handful of coins alongside. He will need to wake the publican upstairs if he's not already aroused by the yelling and noise of falling chairs and tables.

He grabs the taller of his victims, the one by the door, and drags him outside and across the street, sitting him up against the post supporting the horse railing. The man puts up no resistance as he tries to nurse his broken hand, his head and back. He will have a tough walk home when he finally tries. The second robber is more feisty with less damage. But all he can do is offer up meaningless curses against his assailant. Likewise, his hand is broken, his crown jewels will never be the same, and his collarbone may mend if he gets to the right doctor. He grimaces in pain as Mick drags him across the floor and then bundles him over his shoulder to cross the street and deposit him beside his partner. As a final mark of his efforts Mick pulls the boots off both men, walks fifty yards and tosses them high onto the roof of the closest one-storey building.

Rob Bundy, the pub proprietor, is waiting at the front door of his pub, the small pane of glass in his hands.

 "Thanks Mick. If this is my only cost I have much to be grateful for. No real damage to the tables and chairs knocked over. You guys are the best. That pair would have made off with near twenty five pounds if you hadn't been here. Here's five guineas from all of us owners, and remember, the drinks are always free.

"Good night to you my friend."

Note, in the following story, 'stone' is a measure of weight equal to 14 lbs.

Swim Lessons

Business activity has ceased for the day. Even the stand-alone cafes and restaurant rooms have long closed their doors to the public. Now, a cacophony of piano music, laughter, bawdy songs, and drunken shouts rents the late-night air. Pubs full of visitors and thirsty, rowdy, area residents are doing a roaring trade.

While the penal colony's Governor turned the meandering footpaths and lanes of Sydney proper into straightened streets during the 1810s, fifteen years later the narrow roads and alleyways of The Rocks area remain crooked and uneven. This is a community that owns itself and brooks no interference from outside.

The most populous part of Sydney is fiercely managed by the people who live here - free settlers, merchants, sailors, emancipists, and others. The law has little authority in this region that hugs the western shore of Sydney Cove. It's the heart of commercial enterprise in the city, and resourceful developers keep building flats, boarding houses, hotels, pubs, offices, shops, and churches. Demand for living and working space is increasing.

As much as it offers a convenient location, and newcomers find it easy to be assimilated there, the area has a dark side also. Journalists decry it as a slum, where every species of debauchery and villainy is practiced. Their cries are not without reason, for crime and rogue entertainment takes place every night along its thoroughfares.

Where the law won't act however, concerned individuals work to improve the situation.

Drake stumbles through the pub doorway into the night. He grabs one of the frame posts, avoiding a spill onto the dirty boardwalk. The stale smell of beer and tobacco smoke follows him outdoors. Weak lamp light from within casts its glow to the world momentarily, snuffed out as the heavy oak door slams shut behind him, narrowly missing his fingers. He reaches into the pocket of his leather jacket, withdraws a match, and strikes it against the door jam. The incendiary flash is startling in the deep shadows formed by the tin roof of the building's overhang. The spark flares into a small cone of flame as he lights what's left of the cigarette dangling from one side of his mouth.   He limps forward with surprising agility to the edge of the verandah. In the wan light from the sliver of moon overhead his sunken eyes reflect nothing, yet see all.

Two shadows across the street shift in the slight breeze coming off the water. Prostitutes' uncontrolled summer skirts. Drake smirks, grabs at his crotch and loosens his pants which are scrunched tight around well-endowed privates. He wonders if anyone watching can see through his fake stumble and limp, intended to imitate a weak, inebriated customer.

Tilly elbows her companion. "That's him, let's go." Together they silently descend the four rickety steps into the park on the bank of the harbour. The moonlight is mottled through the two huge eucalyptus trees that frame the narrow pathway, failing to downplay the girls' gaudy makeup and provocative clothes. Low-cut cotton blouses reveal large jostling breasts, while the short skirts, rouged cheeks and lips, and bright red fingernails complete the advertisement of their profession.

"I'm scared," Ruby whispers. "Are you sure about this?"

"Someone's got to do it, and it's our turn."

Drake crosses the road haphazardly, avoids the park steps the girls used, falls down over the small parapet and crawls behind one of the trees. His hat is pulled low over his eyes so no light reflects off his forehead. He throws the cigarette stub away, hides his hands in his pockets, and squats out of view of anyone walking along the track by the water's edge. This is his third night on watch. Surely tonight will be his lucky night.

Two young men approach Tilly and Ruby. Drake tenses. The chaps are laughing drunkenly, slapping each other on the back, pushing each other sideways back and forth.   A fairly good looking pair, not old enough to have full beards, but no doubt old enough to entertain themselves using female anatomy.   Drake muses, perhaps sailors just arrived off a ship?   No matter how harmless they look he doesn't relinquish his careful study of the pair. They swagger up to the girls, plainly ogling the generous cleavage offered. Tilly plays along with the banter until she sees enough coins in one of the fellows' hands to make a decision. She turns to Ruby, whispers in her ear, and leaves. The trio saunter off, Tilly between the men, her arms around each of their shoulders, her slender body rubbing up and down against their hips, their arms locked around her skinny waist.

Drake frowns. Must have been more money offered than the usual guinea price for each in order to tempt Tilly away. Ruby watches the three walk off, then turns towards Drake's position, hoping to see an outline of his hat and body shape. To no avail. Her eyes move sideways to the steps and she lets out a scream as a man in dark clothing runs across the lawn brandishing a large kitchen knife. The wavering reflection of moonlight on one side of the knife and then the other strikes terror in her heart.

Drake is on his feet instantly, his great bulk moving at high speed towards the attacker, aiming to intercept the man's route to Ruby who is fleeing in the opposite direction Tilly took. Thoughts race through Drake's mind as he closes on the pursuer. Two decoys sent to goad him into complacence. He should have been suspicious when they purchased services from only one of the girls. He should have kept watch on the stairs, the only pathway in comparative darkness. He should have stood up instead of staying crouched when Tilly left. Bastards. He swears to himself. They'll all pay.

The knife wielding chap gains on Ruby, despite being hampered by the long woolen coat he is wearing. No doubt its pockets are filled with other nasty weapons, such as chains, knuckle dusters, a cosh, maybe a small dagger. Just as he lunges forward with the deadly knife, Drake uses both arms to bring his large solid oak nightstick down on the man's shoulder, breaking his swing and crunching bone.

The intense pain causes the attacker to yell mightily and to drop the knife on the ground as he staggers to a stop. He turns to face Drake, snarls, and with his good arm pulls a long chain from around his waist. He spits in Drake's face and starts to swing the chain above his head. "You are mincemeat, you ugly toad. I'll make a cripple outta you."

Drake looks the braggart square in the eyes and detects a flicker of hesitation, maybe uncertainty. Drake moves forward and knees the man violently in the groin. The arm holding the chain sags and the chap doubles over. Drake drives a pile-driver uppercut directly into the man's chin. The man crumples against the railing, the chain falling on his head as he slides slowly to the ground by the iron fencing along the waterfront, unconscious.

Drake examines the interloper closely. He has no cap covering his unruly black hair, parted on one side. There is a scar leading from under one eye around the top of the cheek to the hairline. Otherwise the face is unremarkable except for thick lips now closed. The clothes are not those of a poor man, although it's possible that they have been stolen. The pants aren't quite long enough and the attacker's boots have different colored laces.

Soft moans come from Ruby who is sitting on the grass ten feet away, sobbing into her handkerchief. Drake is breathing hard but turns to her, "I'll be with you in a minute dearie. Hang on. I need to fix this scum."

He's not done with Ruby's assailant yet. His anger is at full tilt, partially for being duped, partially because he's finally caught up with the guy who has been mutilating prostitutes along the waterfront over the past three months. He sits the chap upright and pulls his right arm under the lower rail then brings it forward above the rail. In quick succession, he breaks every finger on the assailant's right hand, causing outbursts at the intense pain each time. The would-be murderer tries to struggle away but Drake's grip is like a vice, and he keeps his knee pushed upwards into the chap's throat. He repeats the finger breaking performance on the left hand causing his victim to black out a second time.

Drake finally steps back. A small group of male and female onlookers has gathered. Some are silent at the brutal beating handed out. Others, more knowledgeable about the circumstances, grunt approval. One of them voices his feelings, "T'anks Mr. D. Doubt he'll bother any of the girls agin." No one mentions the police. It's their absence and incompetence in The Rocks area that has led to the existence of this group of vigilantes. Drake, known by the single name or the popular pseudonym, is their leader.

He has one last act of vengeance to complete on the now helpless creep at his feet. He reaches down and pulls the man's boots off, followed by his britches. He hands the collection to one of the bystanders and tells him to dispose of the belongings wherever he chooses. The group is laughing at the exposure of the man's genitals and pale legs. To add to their delight Drake jumps with both feet on the man's crown jewels squishing them between the chap's legs and adding a cut to his flopsy member. Even some of the male onlookers gasp at this final violation. The victim splutters and spits a stream of vomit, but is too far gone to fully appreciate his state.

Drake is a virtual giant at 6ft 7in tall and well over 18 stones in weight. He empties the pockets of the attacker's coat, creating a pile of nasty weapons beside the length of chain. He then picks up the attacker, and with a mighty heave, throws him over the railing into the cold waters of Sydney Cove.

He walks back to the lawn, kneels by Ruby, puts his arms around her, and gently says, "I'm sorry dear. I was clumsy. It wasn't meant to happen that way. But thanks to you we've finally caught the murdering bastard. He won't be up to any more strikes I assure you. I'll walk you 'ome. You've had enough excitement for one evening. Then I'll go find Tilly and the boys who dragged her away leaving you vulnerable. Come on."

As they head back to Ruby's flat which she shares with Tilly, Drake asks "Where would Tilly take those boys?"

"Probably to the Anchor and Chain. There's rooms upstairs we 'ave access to. Let me come with you. I want to make sure she's alright."

"OK. That's two blocks away. Are you feeling better? You've had a horrible shock. That chap nearly got you."

"Thanks to you he didn't though. I shudder to think what would have happened had you not been around Drake. All the girls in the neighbourhood will be pleased to hear he's caught. In fact we really should celebrate. There'll be a few other gals at the Anchor and Chain, and I'm sure Roy, the publican, will help arrange a party. Come on, I'm feeling better already. And just to show you I mean it you're welcome to a freebie for saving me. I'll show you how grateful I can be."

"Ha, maybe another night dearie. Thanks anyway. I'm so wound up from beating that chap I might hurt you."

"OK, but I won't forget. Now come on, I need that drink. I'll race you over there."

With that Ruby adds a little speed to her gait, and the incongruous couple hurry to the nearby pub.

****   ****   ****   ****   ****

The celebratory party is in full swing when Tilly leads her two charges downstairs, both smiling happily. Ruby rushes forward and pours out her story. Tilly's hands fly to her mouth as she hears how much danger she left her friend in. She cries, but Ruby wipes away the tears and pulls her along to the small round table where Drake sits with a couple of his comrades.

Drake turns and touches Tilly's cheek. "Glad you are OK gal. I wasn't sure about those two shysters. Where are they? I'm going to have a few words with them and teach them a small lesson."

Tilly speaks up. "Don't hurt 'em Mr. D. They're greenhorn sailors off the convict ship 'Queen's Passage' on its second visit here. Last time was five years ago in 1820 they said. They just got taken in by a seemingly friendly local con artist. Besides which, they are both very well endowed. Young and enthusiastic. No women in four months at sea. They had a lot to offer so to say."

"Still, they need to know patterns of good behaviour. I promise I won't hurt their precious tools in case you see them again. But they need to know what happened. I see them heading for the door, so I'll go make sure they get back to their ship OK."

He winks at his two decoy volunteers, thankful they are not hurt like some of the assassin's other victims. Those still alive that is, scarred with horrible cuts to their faces, breasts and pudenda, no longer attractive in their profession. The police never tried to find the ugly anti-sex crusader, probably scared they could fall victim to his violence also. Drake and his mates decided to take the law into their own hands. So far no-one has tried to stop them.

Outside in the struggling moonlight Drake spies the two men walking in the direction of the wharves where they can get a tender back to their ship. He calls out to them and they stop in their tracks, recognizing the giant in the pub as a friend of the gal they'd just spent nearly an hour with.

"What're yer names?" Drake asks.

"Colin Turnbull."

"Peter Abbott"

"Well you two, you nearly got a sheila killed tonight. How much did that slimy vermin pay you to take her partner away on her own?"

Turnbull responds, "Dunno what you're talkin' about mate. Tilly seemed more anxious than the other sheila, that's all."

"Don't try to bullshit me you little creep. The gals were working as a pair for me and weren't supposed to split up. Wanna try a different answer?"

With that, Drake pulls Abbott down to the ground by the collar on his coat, and steps hard on his throat. While Abbott coughs and squirms trying to free himself, Drake twists Turnbull's arm up behind his back.

He increases the pressure and bellows in Turnbull's ear, "One more time. How much?"

Terrified, Turnbull says, "We got a pound each. Let me go."

"Then fork it over, both of you. You shouldn't be carrying a would-be-murderer's money in any event."

Drake reaches into Turnbull's coat pockets with his free hand and extracts all the coins there. He lets go of Turnbull's arm and turns his attention to Abbott who has given up his struggles.

"You too you little shit. Hand yer money over. This will go to the fund for all the injured ladies in the community." Hurt, and aware of the big man's violent streak, Abbott readily empties his pockets.

He whines, "We need a coin to get rowed out to our ship in the harbour. Spare us that."

"No flamin' way you scum. You can swim to yer ship. Now piss off, and if you ever come back to The Rocks, make sure it's on a night when I'm not around."

The pair turn tail and hurry off towards the wharves. Drake retraces his steps to the Anchor and Chain, a smile on his lips. He muses, "A very good night indeed."

Note, in the following story, the 'Heads' are the north and south bluffs that define the quarter-mile wide entrance to Sydney Harbour from the Pacific Ocean.

Shark Food

Mick and Drake stay hidden 75 yards back from the docks in the little shack that up till a year ago was used for recording the catch. The new hand-held weighing apparatuses have relegated the shack to impotence however. The measurements are now done directly on the wooden slats of the jetties using huge plastic tubs with loopy rope handles.

The two men feel cramped, as old fishing baskets and old cleaning equipment has been discarded into the shed over time, taking up most of the space. They forced themselves into the hut 2 hours ago in the pitch black of night, and both have had to pee in the back corner already, so the place reeks. They grumble yet again about whether the task they face is all worth it, for this is their third early morning shacked up.

As the sun climbs over the treetops on the opposite shore they watch through the fly-dirt and cobweb-covered window. They are pleasantly surprised when the four chaps they've been waiting for saunter down to the benches at the back of the dock. Two are smoking cigarettes, flicking ash onto the boards, caps pulled down just above their eyes. One holds a whip for the two horses attached to the dray that's waiting on the side of the road up the grassy slope from the water's edge. The fourth juvenile flicks the blade on his pocket knife open and shut. Their shirts and slacks are old and dirty, their boots loose and untied. They are louts of the first order, brazenly waiting the return of a laden-down fishing boat. In each of the last two weeks certain fishermen have been robbed of their catch.

Don and his son Charlie feel they will be the next targets to be held up and have hired Drake and Mick to prevent that happening.

When Mick was first approached by Charlie he asked why the fishermen didn't request the police to intervene. The docks weren't in The Rocks area where the police were scared to venture, but in Dawes Point, a far less dangerous spot. The police force was made up of lazy Irish individuals, more interested in being paid protection by pub and store owners. Plus, they only had one man on duty overnight. The other cops didn't start work before 8:30 am. By that time the fish market docks were empty, all the fresh catch having been sold to the city's merchants and restauranteurs.

The fishermen were so disgusted at the lack of interest and help by the police that after the second robbery they decided revenge was in order. A group took a tub full of offal and fish heads uptown and dumped the contents on the main desk at the city police station. The police chased the men but didn't catch any. In the evening the cops turned up in force at the docks as the fishermen prepared to set out for the long night's work, but got a dosing from the hoses, and more fish heads thrown at them. Apparently none of the cops had a yearning to follow the men out to sea.

The fishermen and the dock hands depend on the overnight catch for their livelihood, and the threats the juvenile gang of four present are scary. The gang members held knives at the throats of two of the previous men they robbed, and cut one deeply across the back of his hand. A young lad, no older than ten, had been held as ransom and had had his arm broken when the fishermen would not comply initially with the gang's demands. That act changed things and the thieves got away with two tubs of fish which they later sold on the black market, depressing prices that morning. Immediately after the second robbery, the leaders of the local industry, through Charlie, approached Mick for help.

Which explains why Mick and Drake are ensconced in the foul, cramped little shack, waiting.

Don's longboat comes into view with Charlie at the oars. Nets are rolled up at the stern, and a large canvas bag at the bow is bulging with the night's catch. Some days are more rewarding than others. This looks like a plentiful harvest, most likely including grouper, snapper and black flathead. The food tastes of Sydney citizens are pretty sophisticated, although they demand that their seafood be fresh. Don and Charlie have been out all night, along with several other boats. Theirs is the largest boat to return so far.

The leader of the robbery gang stands on the wharf where Don ties up. "Looks like a good night's haul mister. We'll be happy to help you unload if you like."

Don is no fool. "We're quite able to do that ourselves sonny, so step aside and make room."

"As I said old man, we're here tohelp. I'm not moving."

Don is a big-boned guy, not afraid of a scrap now and then, and on his own the chap doesn't scare him. It's the three others coming up behind their leader that make the foursome too much to handle singly.

He considers his options. "OK, pull me up," and stretches out his arm. "You try anything silly and my son will simply take off."

"Right, I'll change places with you and my friends can help lift that full bag out onto the dock."

The thug reaches out and grips Don's hand, and starts to pull him onshore, but halfway up he lets go and Don falls back into the cold water. Charlie grabs at an oar but the gang leader laughs and jumps into the boat. He yells, "You try to use that mate and you are dead meat." He draws out his knife and flicks the blade open, raising it above his head so it is easily seen. Charlie sits still, seething. His father is sputtering in the water, swimming for the rope ladder twenty yards along the dock.

The knife wielder turns to his fellow gang members but is startled to see two huge men standing quietly behind them. His three friends have been watching events so closely they have no idea that they have company.

Where the hell did they come from their leader wonders. Before he can speak, Drake addresses him. He shouts and the three figures in front of him jump in shock. "Tell you what mister knife man, my friend and I won't hurt your mates here if you climb out of that boat without making a fuss. Sound like a deal?"

One of the three turns as if to run off. Drake hits him in the kidney with a wicked blow from his nightstick and the chap doubles over in severe pain. Mick puts his arms around the necks of the other two and smashes their heads together. They howl in misery, but Mick isn't finished. He knees one of the pair hard in the groin. The chap goes down cursing and clutching his crotch. The other one is dazed, trying to shake the cobwebs in his brain. Mick watches for a second then suddenly drives the heels of his palms on both hands against the chap's ears. The lout is stunned and falls to the hard deck. Drake, meanwhile, has his arm in a choke-hold around his victim's neck.

Mick leaves his two writhing victims and walks to the edge of the dock and addresses the knife man. "So sonny, my partner offered you a deal, but you didn't take it up. He's an impatient guy as you've just seen. Do you want to reconsider things?"

"Screw you fucker, this fisherman here is dead meat," is the response as the knife is waved in the air again. Just as Mick had anticipated. Knowing Drake will take care of the two charges laying on the dock Mick jumps onto the large canvas bag of fish between the two men in the boat. He lands unevenly and the boat wobbles precariously as his weight changes the boat's balance. The gang leader swings his knife but it only rips canvas as Mick rolls out of the way.

He steps back towards where Charlie is stationed, and hisses at his assailant. "I'll give you one last chance to leave this boat you scumbag full of shit."

"Or what you big ox? I'm sure I can run faster than you."

"I've no doubt of that shitbag, although you might find it harder with this."   In an amazingly fast movement, Mick retrieves a knife out of his boot and throws it hard into the arm of his challenger. He follows up by jumping over the canvas bag and punching the chap hard in the stomach. As the lout doubles over, he yelps in pain and Mick adds a crosscut punch to the cheek which silences him totally. Mick retrieves his knife from where it is embedded in a fleshy muscle, wiping both sides on the victim's flannel shirt.

"Hey Drake, wanna take this guy from me so the men can get on with unloading?" Mick hoists the guy up by his armpits and Drake takes over. He sits the beaten-up lout next to his three mates and binds the four together with the long coil of rope he's brought from the shack.

"That was too easy Mick, not much fun at all. But I doubt they've learned their lesson yet. What do you think?"

"I think you're right Drake. Let me help Don and Charlie get their catch on deck before we dream up some nice play games for this little gang."

Don is soaking wet, but is smiling in any event. "We owe you Drake. Thanks for your help."

Charlie shakes Mick's hand. "That's a mean knife throw you have there mister. Were you aiming for his arm or somewhere else?"

"Actually, tell the truth, it was a rotten throw. The boat moved a little as I threw it. I was really aiming for his dick and balls. I must practice some more on a moving platform. Might need to borrow your boat one day."

Charlie smirks. "Shit, glad you're on my side Mick. Would hate to meet you down a dark alleyway. I'd better get on with the sorting. Thanks again."

Drake puts in his spoke. "You guys finished jawing? We've got work to do. Come on Mick."

The four louts on the grass are mouthing off between groans. The guy whose arm was sliced is bleeding steadily from the cut. A small crowd of other fishermen and buyers are gathering around. Cries of 'Good job', 'Well done', 'Kill the scum', and worse are bandied around.

Mick and Drake chat over the heads of the foursome. Drake says, "I don't think anyone wants these chaps able to take fish to the black market again, do you Mick?"

"I'm sure not Drake. I also think many folks would like to see some payback for breaking that little boy's arm. Best thing I can think of is that we break the arm of whatever one of these did it. What do you say?"

The four are now squirming desperately, trying to loosen their bonds, with three of them whimpering like babies. The leader yells, "Let us go. We promise we'll never come back. God's truth. You've made your point. Back off." One of the moaners has soiled his pants, and Mick takes delight in pointing it out to the crowd. "He must be the one who did the kid, look he's shit scared already." Mick reaches down and picks the lout up by his ears and shakes him. The lout screams as Drake unties him from his mates.

Mick applies pressure to the chap's right hand between his thumb and adjacent finger. He raises the hand to his own chest and breaks the thumb by pushing forward. The man screams. Mick bends the guy's wrist 90 degrees with his fingers pointing up, places his other forearm under the guy's elbow and pressures the wrist downward until there's a sickening snap. The guy screams and his arm hangs uselessly. Some in the crowd are shocked at the speed with which things just happened. Others yell 'Got what he deserves', 'that's justice' and other supporting words.

Drake doesn't stand on niceties, He grabs the leader's right hand and quickly breaks each finger one by one. Before they realize he's attacking them the remaining two louts get their fingers broken as well. Drake bellows to the watchers, "Well gents I think that takes care of them trying to steal any more fish for a few years. You have any trouble with anyone else don't hesitate to get in touch. You know where to find us."

He turns to walk away but Mick stops him, and addresses the fishermen. "Did I overhear one of you say you saw a shark inside the Heads this morning?" A scraggy older chap at the fringe of the crowd responds. "That was me, I tried to catch him but he slipped away. Right off Manly cove was where he was, a couple of miles out from here."

"Are you all finished unloading old-timer?" Mick asks.

"Yep, about to head home to the missus. You guys done good, we all thank ye."

"Wait, before you go, would you be willing to row me out 200 yards to the middle of the cove here?"

"Could do. What for?"

"Well, this little gang's major shitbag leader is still bleeding from his arm. I thought if we dropped him in the water out there he might learn to swim in a hurry, even with a broken hand. Someone once told me sharks have an incredible sense of smell, especially of blood in the water."

A new voice from the middle of the crowd responded. "Let me do it. Was my boy whose arm was broken."

"OK mister. You're on. Show me your boat and I'll bring this little shit by."

The gang leader starts screaming his head off, so Drake backhands him across the mouth hard enough to make the chap's lips swell and his teeth bite his tongue. The cries cease immediately.

Drake turns to Mick. "He's all yours mate. I'll take the other three back to their dray, and they can wait to see if their leader returns. See ya later."

Note, in the following story, the monetary unit 'one shilling' was often colloquially called 'a bob'. A 'dilly-bag' is a bag made from the fibres of certain plants by the Aborigines.

One Shilling

"I've been looking for you two. You're not easy to find."

The old chap pulls off his hat, scratches the top of his head, and sits down on the grass three feet away from the pair he's addressing. Drake and Mick turn to look more closely at the man. Ordinary looking fellow – maybe just under 6 feet tall, dirty dungarees tied with rope at the waist, pants lapping strong leather boots. A nondescript shirt and waistcoat, unbuttoned, facial features somewhat gaunt but at the same time not unfriendly.

"Who's been looking then?" Drake responds.

"Tom Easterman."

"Where you from Tom? Haven't seen you round here before."

"Other side of the harbour. Rowed me dinghy to the Quay. Don't do that much anymore."

"You look strong enough."

"Older than I look sonny.   You got anything to eat? Didn't eat since yesterday."

Mick, reaches in a small sack by his side. "How about an apple?   Here you go."   He tosses it across the intervening space where it's well caught.

"Thanks bunches. Glad I found you. Need your help."

Mick is all sympathy. "Better tell us your story friend. What's up?"

"Do you know the place called Manly?"

"Heard the name. New community out near the Heads somewhere, right? That where you from?"

"You got it.   Gonna be a great place eventually. No more than 100 people there yet. Several coves on the harbour protected from most winds. Keeps me boat in one of them. Strip of land is a peninsula which leads out to the north head. Lots of bush. But 350 yards from one of the coves is a beautiful beach washed by the Pacific. Nothing like it anywhere in the harbour. Rolling waves, pure white sand. Only the seagulls and the sharks know it. "

Drake interrupts. "OK, OK.   We're hardly the beach types mate. What's it to us?"

"Well, I want you to come back there with me."

"What for? Doubt there's anything there we need."

"We have a problem you could help us with."

"What sort of problem you talking about, and who's the 'we' you mention?"

"Small group of us concerned about our womenfolk. Problem is not pleasant."

Drake stands, shuffles his feet, restless. "Only women we know here are barmaids and prostitutes. Oh, and Sally the baker. They get our protection sometimes. Is that what you're wanting?   Do you have a pub and bakery in Manly?"

"Just one general store at the moment."

"Come on Tom, old-timer. What's the problem?"

"Nasty. There's this wild bushman. Has raped two women from the community. Waits till they head to the bush or to a privy to relieve themselves, then accosts them. Apparently he's either part aborigine or is an escaped convict who's lived with the aborigines. Carries a dilly-bag and a spear. Is very dark skinned, comes barefoot, wears nothing but a loincloth, smells awful, is wiry but powerful, vanishes afterwards among the trees, impossible to track. Holds the spear against the women's throats then cuts their tits before leaving."

Drake hangs his head. "Aww shucks. Sorry to hear this. Definitely, a nasty piece of work, as you say. Am sure all the women are scared. But why don't you ask the police for help and have them bring along a tracker?

"Police won't come to Manly. Too far away. And the rotten Irish pigs that they are we don't want them anyway. Their abo trackers might be good at following white men convicts who've escaped but from what we hear they never catch up with anyone from their own tribes."

Mick weighs in. "Think you're about right there matey. But Drake and me aren't any good at tracking, that's for sure. Never even tried to do it. We're city boys. We'd be useless trying to find and catch the guy in the forests where he's at home. Doesn't make sense. I've heard abos can become part of the shadows among the trees if they want. And who's to say he doesn't have mates to help hide him and even attack pursuers?"

"Wait a minute lads. Two things. First, there are friendly natives in the area. At least a couple of families. We've traded ears of corn for fish they catch. Those folks seem harmless enough. They leave their nawis pulled up on the beaches. We don't touch them and they don't touch our dinghies."

"What are 'nawis'?

"That's what they call their bark canoes. Amazing vessels made out of a single piece of bark stripped from a giant stringybark gum tree, fired, and bent into shape. Amazing little boats. When the first fleet arrived back in 1788 they called our ships 'mawi nawi' – meaning 'big canoe.' How the women balance those things out on the water is incredible to watch."

"Yeah, but they still have their spears and woomeras right? Do they leave those with their boats?"

"No, and neither do we leave our guns with ours. The point is there are friendly abos around. We even try to teach each other our two languages. We think this wild bushman is a loner, not one of the local Gamaragal tribe members. He probably lives near them, not exactly with them."

"So you know where this tribe lives?"

"Not specifically. Once when a couple of us tried to walk back with some of the fisher-folk to their camp they made it clear it was not to be. We've seen smoke rising through the trees a mile or so away. That's all."

Drake takes over the dialog. "You mentioned there was a second thing to tell us."

"We're all pretty scared. The women even have to wait till a man's around to escort them to the vicinity of the privy. They all live in fear of being attacked by the guy. Could be if some woman has an urgent need and can't wait, that she could become the next victim. We have to assume the guy is watching from the depths of the forest most of the time, waiting for another opportunity. It's possible he's watching from up in a tree somewhere. We simply have no idea how to find him in his own environment.

"But, we have a half-baked idea about how we might catch the shit. Not sure how smart it is or how realistic we're being. But there's a young chap in our midst who's mighty angry about the bushman. His wife is one of the women who got raped. Bob Patterson is his name. He thinks he could dress up as a woman and set a trap for the guy. Actually he's one of the skinnier guys around. Thinks he could shave his beard and mustache off and wear one of his wife's dresses, and shove a couple of apples under his singlet for tits. His feet are too big for ladies' boots, and since his legs are almost hair-less he'd just go barefoot. He could wear one of his wife's bonnets to complete the ruse.   Far from perfect, but the notion is he'd go outdoors to the woods and squat to pee, just after dusk when the light has faded, making it hard for the bushman to see details from his hiding place. What do you think?"

"Damned risky if you ask me," Mick replies. "Even if the bushman is fooled from a distance, who knows what he'll do when he gets close and finds out his mistake. Could easily kill this chap Bob. Gutsy guy to suggest it. Gotta applaud his willingness to try."

"I think we all know that, which is why I'm here. You see, everyone over in Manly has heard about you two. They know you're afraid of nothing, handy with fists and boots, give no mercy, hurt or maim yet do not kill. The Christians in the community like that bit, although not 100% sure about the extent of beatings. They want enough to dissuade the rogue from visiting again, that's all.   Plus, I should add, we're willing to pay you for helping us out.   We thought if you were well hidden nearby where Bob goes, you could capture the chap if and when he appears close up."

Mick and Drake are silent. They retreat up the grassy slope. Their reputation for keeping The Rocks area free of the worst type of offenders is one thing. They have personal motivation, as it's where they live.   Applying their efforts in another part of Sydney is something else however. They're somewhat surprised their work is known as far away as Manly. But pleased as well. The pair look at each other and Mick nods his acquiescence to Drake. "I'm willing to give it a go mate, if you are."

"Yeah me too, and I thought of something else. Rosie, the pro who works out of the Ball and Chain pub. She told me once that she managed to bring some of her little extras with her from London – a really short skirt, pads to make her tits look bigger, and a wig with blond pigtails. How she got them here is open to the imagination. But I wonder if she'd at least loan us her wig for this Bob character. Better than just a bonnet methinks."

'You have a smart memory Drake, for sure. But Rosie will be sleeping off her worknight right now. Don't think she'd love us too much if we go wake her."

"Let's see what Tom thinks."

They catch up with Tom who's munching on another apple pulled from Mick's bag. Drake winks at him and says, "OK mate. We'll give it a go. And we have an idea."

After telling Tom about Rosie's wig, Drake asks him whether he can take them all back across the harbour in the dark. Tom looks around, walks up the little grassy knoll and spies the moon rising in the east. It's about quarter size, and since there are no clouds, he has no problem with the notion of navigating back to Manly later.

Tom shows his new friends where his boat is tied up, and the trio agree to meet there around 10 pm.

Drake arrives with Rosie's wig wrapped carefully in a clean canvas bag. She sends her wishes that the rapist be caught and dealt with appropriately. And, that nothing happen to her wig, even though she no longer uses it. "Sentimental value" is her only reason.

The journey along and across the harbour takes longer than Mick and Drake expect. Their macho reputations demand that they show no concern, but both are uncomfortable being on the water with no means to help themselves should they capsize. They both fear having to become swimmers and silently will Tom to make the trip as smooth as possible. The moon shines directly in their eyes, highlighting the wavelets they forge through. After an hour Tom turns and points out a couple of lights on Manly's harbour beach and warns the pair that the ride is about to become rocky and scary while they broach the swell coming from the

Pacific Ocean as it forces its way into the harbour between the north and south Heads.

Drake's stomach reacts negatively to the rapid rise and fall of the boat and its lopsided movements rolling left and right. His dinner is ejected into the dark waters, and his face drains of color, unseen in the wan moonlight. Mick does better by holding his head between his knees, but both are tremendously relieved when they finally enter the sheltered portion of the cove and Tom glides them to a beach stop. They help him pull the boat well above the high-tide mark and tie the rope painter to an iron post buried deep in the sand.

It's warm enough for the two avengers to sleep on the beach near a group of men who are gathered around a smoky driftwood fire. Tom tells the group who he has brought with him, and the members assure Tom they'll keep watch over the newcomers. Tom heads to his modest home and worried wife who has been waiting his return for hours. Hubbie's details about the help he's brought diminishes her angst. She looks forward to sharing the news throughout the community on the morrow.

Early the next morning Tom walks Mick and Drake around the settlement introducing them to the residents. They are shown where the two women were attacked and where Bob Patterson proposes to act as decoy. After lunch Tom, Bob, and the two newcomers develop a plan for the evening and Bob dresses up in his female outfit and adds the blonde wig. The three onlookers laugh but give a grudging OK as to how well Bob comes off. Drake has brought an extra knife with him which Bob straps around his left thigh, hidden from view under the dress.

In case the wild man arrives in the vicinity before nightfall, Drake and Mick stay inside Bob's hut, while Bob goes about his regular activities, preparing his boat for a night fishing episode. The other residents also try to act as normally as possible, wanting nothing to get in the way of Bob's ruse. Of course there's no guarantee that the bushman will even turn up but it's been 10 days since the previous attack, matching the time interval between the first and second incidents, so Bob and the others are hopeful.

Bob makes his guests a dinner of local snapper, washed down with a glass of South African wine. Mick double checks. "Bob, are you sure you want to do this? I'd be happy to go in your place, although I'm sure I wouldn't look as pretty." He smiles as he utters the last few words.

"I'm fine Mick, but I appreciate the offer and feel good with you two being so close by. I just hope the bastard turns up."

On the mantle above the fireplace Drake notices an old hand-bell. "Bob, that bell may be worth taking along. In case the guy creeps up from behind and puts his hand across your mouth to stop you yelling you could ring that bell to let us know he's with you. We'll be watching, but if he does move like a shadow we might have a hard time seeing him anyway."

"Smart thinking Drake. You're right. With the women, he approached from the side, poking them with his spear, then grabbed them by the throat with his huge hands. I'll keep the bell hidden as best I can. If he is a true abo he won't know what it is, but if he's a convict turned native, he probably would know."

On the inside of the door to the hut a coiled-up whip serves as decoration. Drake wonders if it could be useful. "Where'd the whip come from Bob?" he asks.

"When I lived in Paramatta I used to catch cod in the freshwater river running down from the mountains. One day a hungry bullock drover traded it for a small barrel of fish I had left over. It's just a memento from a time when me and the missus first set up lodgings away from Sydney. You're welcome to use it if you want."

"Might come in handy methinks. I've handled whips before so know how to use it. Thanks."

The afternoon hours drift by agonizingly slowly, but as soon as it is dark enough to light a lamp, Bob walks back and forth across the large living cum dining room throwing his silhouette against the sheet over the window facing the woods.

An hour passes. Mick rubs his face, neck, forehead and hands with old charcoal embers to hide his light skin and slips out of the hut, making his way to Bob's neighbour's house where the owners have deliberately lit no lamps. Mick doesn't stay, quickly exiting through a second door which opens three feet from a large eucalyptus at the edge of the tree line. He drops to his stomach and slithers 15 feet to a pre-determined spot in a direction opposite to that leading to the location of the aborigine camp. He sits up and leans against a stout tree trunk, adjusting his eyesight to the surroundings.

A few minutes later, Bob carefully lifts the bell off the shelf above the fireplace and grabs the ringer with his left hand. Drake opens the outside door and shakes Bob's other hand. "Good luck mate. You're a brave man. We'll be listening closely. Let's hope he takes the bait. Remember, tiptoe like a girl..."

Mick listens to the rustle of the leaves above him, and watches Bob emerge from his house. When the door closes, the yellow patch of light across the ground disappears and the space becomes dark again. A sliver of light from the moon casts large tree shadows across the clearing.

Bob concentrates on his gait, trying to take what he considers dainty-type steps way shorter than his usual stride. He looks ahead towards the place he chose earlier as his potential encounter spot. It is almost in the centre of a ring of trees, selected deliberately, with the notion that if he is attacked and there is a fight from which the assailant tries to run off, the closeness of the trees may cause some hesitation, slowing the abo's flight down a tad.

Drake feels frustrated. Outside it is dark. Yet he sits in lamplight, away from the action, only his ears playing any role. He desperately hopes to hear Bob's bell so he can rush out and engage with the bushman.

Mick turns his head a few degrees to the right. Had he seen a movement or were his senses just toying with him? He holds his breath, willing whatever changed to repeat itself. The lower branches of a tree near Bob's house sway in a small wind gust, and the rustling leaves sound a little louder. False alarm. Mick breathes normally again.

His head swivels back in the reverse direction and he watches as Bob nears his target spot. Twenty feet beyond he spies a shadow flitting between two tree trunks. He forces his eyes to open wider. Surely that was a definite movement. Not some sapling swaying in the breeze. Yes, another shadow leaves one tree and advances across a two foot gap to another tree. The bushman is clearly present! No question.

Mick leans forward and retrieves the hunting knife from its sheath in his right boot. He grips it in a ready-to-throw handle down position. Bob reaches his spot and squats, hiking the front of his dress above his knees.

Suddenly his head jerks back as the bushman rushes up behind, kneels down and pulls his spear handle back against Bob's throat. Instinctively Bob reaches up with his right hand to try and push the spear handle away. His left hand reaches for the bell. He gets three full rings off before letting it go and reaching for the spear handle which is nearly choking him.

The sound of the bell startles the bushman. He makes a fierce guttural sound, and stands up, bending forward to look at the bell, now lying at Bob's feet. Drake grabs the whip and tears out of Bob's hut yelling at the top of his voice. "Got you scumbag. Don't try to get away." The bushman is distracted. He drops his spear and turns to flee. That's when he finds Mick advancing from the side and only 6 feet away.

Bob reaches up to try and grab the bushman's ankle, but misses. Mick throws his knife hard, and its sharp tip lodges tight in the bushman's right thighbone. Mick sees a small spurt of blood as the man lets out an animal-type howl. He's hurt and stunned, but decides to keep moving. After three steps he stops and attempts to pull the knife from his wound. Mistake. He howls again as the knife does not budge. The hesitation allows Drake to catch up and grab the man's left arm. The man squirms to release Drake's grip, but to no avail. He changes tactics and swings his right arm at Drake's head. The knuckles in his closed fist deliver a stinging hit to the temple, forcing Drake to release his grip. The blow makes him stagger back.

Mick reaches forward but his hands slip off the bushman's torso which feels greasy. Mick swears mightily and yells, "I'm going to scramble your brains you shit," and stumbles after the man. Bob yells, "Lookout Mick," and throws the man's spear at his assailant's fleeing back. It's hard to see clearly in the darkness, but it's not hard to hear another wild howl and the crashing of the man's body to the ground.

The spear is lodged beneath the chap's lowest left rib. Drake pulls it out and jumps on the black man's back, pinning him down. Mick pulls the man's feet together and ties them with a length of rope he's been carrying. The man still struggles with fear-ridden strength, so

Drake puts a headlock on him and squeezes hard. The man's screams go raspy and eventually stop. His head lolls as he's rendered unconscious. Bob watches, his yellow dress and wig incongruous in the setting.

Drake turns around, releasing the choke-hold. "Bob, are you OK?"

"Throat's a little sore damn him, and I'm sure glad you suggested that bell. He sure came out of nowhere. I didn't hear a thing."

Mick says, "I saw him move at the last minute but he was on you almost before I stood up. Fast, tricky creep. Let's pull him down to the beach where we can see him in the direct moonlight. I must say, he sure does stink, just like the women said. I want to vomit when I think of him on top of them."

In five minutes the rogue is stretched out on the sand. He's bleeding from two wounds, but not copiously. The blood pools and seeps into the sand. He's just as the women described, wiry, but not looking very vital at the moment.

"Bob, I think it's time for you to go home to your sweet wife and change your clothes. You are a very brave man. The members of your community should all be very thankful and proud of you."

"Well, I do admit I feel a little shaky. Thanks to you both for rescuing me. Looks like he's coming around. Sure you don't want me to stay and help with him?"

"Nope, you head off Bob. Mick and I have unfinished business with the guy. We'll see you later. Cheers."

Bob lopes off, his swaying dress and pigtails bringing smiles to the faces of the duo left behind. "OK Mick, let's first sit him up against that palm tree and tie him neck and stomach so he can't move an inch. I'm dying to see how good my aim is."

The bushman struggles against the ropes in vain. He yells unrecognizable sounds. His head is noosed at his forehead and neck, his body strapped tight under his armpits and hard across his abdomen. He yells his ferocious animal howl again. Mick covers his ears. "I hate that sound." He checks along the shoreline and finds a large crab shell which he shoves in the man's mouth. The yells cease. The white of the man's eyes show eerily from his face. He doesn't cower but stares vehemently at his captors.

Drake measures out 8 short paces from the man's outstretched feet and unfurls the whip. He turns and cracks the leather thong towards the waves. The sound is sharp and shrill, overriding the soft lapping sounds of the waves fading into the sand. "Ah, knew I hadn't lost my touch. Now let's see how good my aim is."

He faces the rapist and hisses at him. Summoning up his disgust and anger he cracks the whip again and a piece of the bushman's left ear drops to the sand, blood following it. The resultant stinging sensation rocks the bushman, and his eyes blink up and down as incredible pain travels across his visage. He utters a shallow whimpering sound that Drake interprets as a request for no more.

Drake moves a foot to his left. Another sharp crack and the bushman's right ear is shattered. It's almost severed through, just a bunch of flesh left dangling. The bushman's face contorts in incredible pain and surprise. Drake coils the whip and rests it over his shoulder.

"I'm done Mick. Your turn me lad."

'Remind me never to step in your way when you're holding a whip mate. Those were two excellent slices. I don't think he'll forget you. Now I do have a favour to ask. Would you mind making him unconscious again for me. I think he's pretty close but I'd like to be certain."

"No problem Mick." Drake walks up to the man's feet, studies him for five seconds, then delivers a super hard kick with his boot under the man's chin. Despite the ropes tying him to the tree the chap's head jerks up then falls down and rocks slightly to his right. He's out cold.

Mick retrieves the bushman's spear and uses it to cut through the dirty loincloth around his hips. He pulls the chap's old rag totally off, walks to the water's edge and drops it into an outgoing wave. "Not much of a prick on him Drake."

"Enough to hurt those two women. Bastard that he is. I have no sympathy for him whatsoever. Am half tempted to hold him down under a wave and drown him. Wouldn't take much. But this way he'll live with his injuries and be known by them forever. Couldn't happen to a nicer guy."

Mick walks back and kicks the man's legs apart. Between them he drives the spear down into the man's dick cutting it three quarters through. The head swings to one side and a trickle of blood emerges. The spear sticks straight up in the sand.

Mick steps back, and the pair debate whether to loosen the bonds tying him to the tree so he can work himself free or to leave him there so villagers and natives alike can see him in the morning. Mick reminds Drake how Tom had said the local Christians didn't really want to know the extent of whatever treatment they handed out. On that note they undo the ropes around the chap's neck, forehead, and chest but break all the fingers on his right hand so he'll have difficulty loosening the last ropes and throwing any spear in the future.

As they walk back to Bob's hut Mick asks "What do you think our simple efforts are worth to these folks Drake? They said they'd pay us."

"Yeah, I know they did, but I consider getting rid of vermin like that guy a sort of public service. But since they'll want to give us something, how about a couple of ears of fresh corn, and a nice big meaty fish. If they insist on coins as well, let's just say one bob, it would be small keepsake to treasure."

"Got you. Agreed. Fish, corn and a bob it is."

————————————————

And in case you missed the deliberate play on words back there, say quickly, "A 'bob it is". Now, check out the Bobbit incident in 1993. Subtle I admit.

London, England, 2012

Table of Contents

Olympic Revenge

Her desperate kick of the black and white ball immediately changed the situation from one of defense to one of offense. She let out a long exultant breath. It had been too darned close. In the previous three minutes their opponents had attacked with more gusto than usual, showing some very clever moves that had allowed them to penetrate towards goal better than any previous attack. Sprawled on the ground where she had slid to kick the ball away from their striker she watched as her teammates moved away up-field. The score was even in a hard fought match. She felt good at helping turn the tide, if only momentarily. Relieved at the current lack of pressure she got up and started to run diagonally to the right flank, watching the play further forward near the left boundary.

Too late out of the corner of her right eye a dark pink mass registered its ugly intention as a fist pounded into her eyeball and forehead. 'What was this?' she thought. In shock she slumped to the ground, courtesy of an opponent's deliberate and vicious hit. Her eye clouded over and a lump immediately started to swell above her eyebrow. Pain raced across her face. The referee and linemen were twenty five yards away managing the game out of sight of the punch. Her attacker ran off while she writhed on the ground. She was conscious of her mind wavering – the grass seemed suddenly greener and the dirt smell was pungent. Her cleats seemed too close and her breath caught as nausea invaded her sensory glands. As quickly as she had nearly blacked out, she suddenly recovered, fully aware of what had transpired. As she sat up trying to rid herself of a dazed dizziness she fought back an immediate urge to chase her adversary and strangle her. She sat for a few more seconds with her head in her hands regaining composure, then decided to rejoin her comrades in even tougher defense.

When a substitute was sent on she thankfully left the field to the cheers of the crowd, and had the trainer check her over. She winced as he placed ice on the mound over her eye, but after a few minutes rest sent her back to join the melee. The see-saw battle continued but she kept well away from her attacker and rejoiced with her teammates when they scored another hard-earned goal and left the field triumphant. She refused to shake hands with her attacker but bore her swelling with pride as the team celebrated their win, moving them forward to the next round.

The overt action of the sucker punch on the field had angered many team fans and after the game they gathered near the competitors' hotel bus taunting and decrying what should have been recognized as a blatant foul earning a red card and possible suspension. Replays on TV during the evening readily validated the unnecessary and unsportsmanlike attack.   Only Janelle really knew how hard she'd been hit.

Paul Denning had been an observer at the game – women's soccer was one sport he could enjoy relaxing at as spectator. Yes, Janelle's teammates were physical, but not in a threatening manner. They were well disciplined, and relied on skill, smarts, fitness, and opportunism to win their games. They had an appetite for playing hard in the sense of giving all they could, but enjoying their matches as well.   He did not like to see any member of the team taken advantage of.   Of any team actually.   In fact he hated seeing anyone taken advantage of, in sports or life, and his crusade to rectify things anonymously gave him great satisfaction. He prided himself on his unadvertised vigilante status.

Out at the bus loading zone, he noted the name of the hotel where the losing team was staying and since it was early evening already he found his motorbike in the parking lot and followed the directions his GPS system gave him, arriving just as the team bus pulled away from the hotel entrance.   He parked in a public garage two blocks further along the street, took his satchel to the nearest public toilet and adjusted his outfit to jeans and long-sleeve shirt, a fashionable sweater, and a beret jauntily perched slantwise on his short dark hair.

He was hoping the girls would freshen up then come back downstairs for a meal in the hotel dining room or at a nearby restaurant that they could walk to. He'd noticed several cafes and other eateries in the area with cuisines ranging from standard British fare in pubs to exotic Asian and South American offerings. Since the team was from South America he bet himself they'd opt for Asian or British food to enjoy something different. He casually strolled along the alleys behind the various shops noting obstacles and semi-hidden passageways should he need to use them.

Of course it was also possible the girls would grab a taxi and head somewhere else on the other side of town. It wouldn't be the first time his instincts had been off. But a few casual comments made as the girls left the soccer arena boarding their bus made him think this would be a 'stay-close-to-the-hotel' evening. They hadn't sounded very upbeat and party-ish. Although from experience he knew that could change with a short rest, hot shower, and the sighting of a sassy dress patiently waiting on a hanger for action.

He wandered through the shops in the hotel arcade, not very high-end ones, but offering a range of pleasant merchandise from men's and women's clothes, to jewelry, souvenirs and sundries. Just as he reached the far end, he heard a babble of high-pitched Spanish and saw a group of players in the hotel foyer, clearly discussing where they should go. The foyer was spacious with several large columns supporting a lighted, domed ceiling and walls of dark oak with paintings of old London adding color. It was friendly and not overly pretentious, one of many similar hotels throughout the city.

The girls were in jeans and comfy blouses and sweaters so it didn't look like they were planning a heavy night out on the town. After consultation with the Concierge and some noisy discussion, three distinct groups formed and headed for the front door. Paul followed them out and crossed the road to observe less conspicuously where they were headed. His target, whose name he had learned was Estella, was in a group of four that strolled animatedly in the direction of a pub whose name Paul recognized from their conversation – about two and a half blocks away. There was a fast food outlet in the same direction but they had clearly decided that sampling some British steak and kidney pie, or fresh trout, might be more to their tastes.

Moving quickly he forged through the pedestrian crush, used a subway entrance to cross back under the street, and entered the pub before they reached the closest street corner. The place was not yet packed as the street lights were only now coming on as the first vestige of darkness arrived. From the accents he heard around the tavern it wasn't just locals who were enjoying the old world ambience and camaraderie. A darts game was going on in one corner, and a TV with re-runs of the day's sporting events in another corner. The place smelled deliciously of pipe smoke and spirits. Large glass mugs of beer were passed through small thongs, and hands wrapped carefully around glasses of Scotch on small table stands. Fierce debates and discussion ranged from solving world problems to analysis of the latest antics on the floor of parliament to predictions for the next weekend's football matches and the next day's Olympic events.

Paul hadn't been in a pub for a while and this brought back warm memories from the time when an Eton schoolboy had to be helped realize his place in the world.   He grinned to himself at the thought of the chap's single sculls taking on water and leaving him floundering in the middle of the Thames. Some folk needed to be publicly embarrassed to realize how it felt when they became the subject of ridicule, and were on the opposite side of humiliation they had previously handed out. Others needed to be hurt for messages to sink in, while others didn't deserve to stay around at all.

The girls entered and it didn't take long for the population of single males to notice their presence. The girls had curves in the right places but they weren't pronounced, as these young ladies were serious athletes.   They just exuded health, vitality, and self-assuredness. Which made them immediately attractive. Space was made at the bar by friendly men, and the message soon spread that these girls were from one of the teams that had played earlier that afternoon. When their identification brought notice that they had lost their game they were offered drinks from multiple corners. The general notion was that pitchers of ale would help them forget about losing and console them very quickly.

As a group they were smart enough to realize drink is absorbed better with food, and after repeated attempts to retain them at the bar they were eventually led to a table in the restaurant. It was at this point that Paul realized he faced a dilemma. How to teach his target a lesson? Wait until dinner was over and try to isolate her somehow on the way back to the hotel, or hope she had to visit the restroom here at the pub and get her then?

He figured she was probably rooming with another team member so trying to get her in a room alone was not likely to work. He hated not having a plan, and usually didn't operate without one. There were far more risks of getting caught when he had to act on an impromptu basis. He liked scoping everything out in advance, determining alternatives, calculating options, checking the environment ahead of time, knowing escape routes, planning changes of clothes or disguise, understanding the local patterns of behavior of the citizens and authorities.

But in this instance he probably would never see Estella again and a lesson had to be provided. He made his way to the men's room and noted with satisfaction that true to old British style, it was a 'one-holer', on one side of the hall by the back door, with the women's directly opposite.   How   these   places   got   away   without upgrading facilities he'd never understand. And then it dawned on him. Of course, there was another restroom near the entrance to the restaurant.   Not as well marked, almost looking like an entry way to the kitchen itself. The maître d' stood behind a little lectern at the main dining room doors partially blocking easy access to the second set of restrooms.

No way for him to control which passage Estella would choose, if she even needed to go.   He'd just have to wait and see. Not that it took long. The girls studied the menu, sipping the drinks they'd brought from the bar. They placed orders for appetizers but kept the menus, indicating they still had to choose a main course.   Two of them pulled their chairs back, one clutching her purse, Estella purse-less. Luck was in. The maître   d'   pointed   Estella's   companion   to   the passageway behind him, while he directed Estella back out through the main bar and lounge area.

Paul disengaged himself from his vantage point near the darts game and quickly crossed the floor to be immediately behind Estella as she elbowed through the crowd. There were now enough new patrons that space was becoming limited and she had to walk around several groups. Concentrating on the path forward she had no sense of Paul's proximity.

The hall turned right ninety degrees then back left in a few paces. This was it he thought. Now or never. No-one else was in the corridor. They were just two drinkers headed to the bathrooms. Estella stopped as she noticed the 'engaged' sign and before she knew what was happening Paul had stuffed his beret in her mouth, grabbed both her arms and propelled her out the back door using his weight to press the open-and-close bar.

His 6 ft 5 inch frame and 200 lbs of lean muscle had little trouble managing the girl. As she struggled to pull an arm free he half turned her and kneed her viciously in the stomach, causing her to double over and retch, his beret dropping underneath her vomit. Her eyes glazed over and he kneed her again, so she had no breath left to yell. He now took her right hand and in a fast, smooth motion quickly bent her little finger sideways breaking it as close to where the finger met the hand as possible. Almost before the pain registered in Estella's mind he grabbed the middle finger of the same hand and bent it back in one quick deliberate movement. The cracking sound left him satisfied, as she now yelled in pain, writhing on the ground. Her eyes looked up at him, questioningly, and she spat out "No mas punzones."

As much as he understood the request he reached down, lifted her face by pulling up her hair and swung his fist hard, landing a fierce blow at her left eye. Perhaps now she'd realize why she had been attacked.

He grabbed his fouled beret and quickly ran off, turning left down an alley, as the rear door of the pub opened and he heard multiple voices yelling in a mixture of concern and anger. His motorbike was some distance away in the public garage, a good block on the other side of the hotel. Highly anxious to be out of the vicinity he ran when no-one else was around, then slowed to a fast walk, throwing the beret and his sweater into a grimy dumpster behind a car repair business.

Long ago he'd learned to put emotions behind him. He still didn't like hurting women, and he'd deliberately left her with only two broken fingers. She'd be in limited pain for six to eight weeks if they were re-set properly, longer if not. The punishment, as he thought of it, wasn't meant to stop her playing soccer, it was to make her think twice about ever hitting anyone again. She'd punched a totally unsuspecting opposing player hard, without any warning or any real reason that he could see. And while the girl she had grounded was smart enough not to retaliate, his codes of behavior and right and wrong said no-one should get away with action like that.

Maybe there were others like him in the world, but his notion of an eye for an eye was something he believed in. Too bad the world in its weakness had given up the belief so many years ago.

The incident made page three of the morning newspapers, buried behind far more meaningful competitive results. His message was not lost on the editors who made repeat references to online versions showing the original knock-out punch Estella had delivered.

Paul was sure that had it been a member of the UK team that had been floored the outcry would have been much larger. Online, comments varied from disgust at his retaliatory actions to carefully worded support of the payback. Police were looking for him, but realized in a city full of visitors at the moment they would have a difficult time catching him. All Estella could tell them was that he was tall, strong, and spoke passable Spanish. Her fingers were reset and she anticipated going home the next day. In interviews she offered no apologies for her action, claiming the other team had been 'overly physical' in their play. Her victim refused to comment, saying she was busy focusing on the next game, and not looking backward.

All very satisfactory, thought Paul. He was in London for a totally different reason and the timing with the Olympics was somewhat coincidental.

Story based on an incident in the 2012 Olympic Games London where Colombian player Lady Andrade sucker punched America Abby Wambach. See

http://www.dailymail.co.uk/news/article-2180632/London-Olympics-2012-Soccer-star-Abby-Wambach-gets-sucker-punched-eye-Colombian-opponent-Lady-Andrade-suspended.html

Don't look at me that way

It is five minutes before 2pm on Saturday 25 February, 2017, the scheduled time for Michael Ayoade to be released through the exit gate of Pentonville Prison. The guards inside will be glad to see him go after four years' incarceration, as the place is overcrowded with local criminals, way more than the prescribed 1300 occupants, and he's been a rabble rouser, so no early release.

Greg watches for the prisoner's presence from a recessed doorway across the road.

A single black female stands rocking backwards and forwards on her heels about twenty-five yards outside the gate, on the pathway that leads to the street sidewalk. Greg figures she must be a girlfriend waiting for Ayoade, as no other inmate is due for release before 2:30pm. The girl arrived just fifteen minutes ago, walking down Caledonian Road from the direction of the tube station, no more than five minutes away. Greg is thankful for the fact she is alone, as it makes his intended task easier. If she'd come by car, or there'd been more friends waiting, things would become far more awkward.

Four minutes after 2pm, two guards exit the side door to the prison building and beckon to someone behind to follow them. It isn't hard to recognize Michael, although he's clearly lost some weight. Prison diets are not known to make you fat. The woman waves enthusiastically, and a grin, visible even across the road, lightens Michael's face.

The couple embrace, and the woman puts her arm in his and they slowly head north back towards the tube station. At Brewery Road they cross Caledonian and Greg breathes another sigh of relief. Their route is just as he had hoped. Michael wants to be as far away from the prison buildings as quickly as possible.

Leaving his watching post, Greg moves quickly to catch up close behind the couple. They pause at the prison bus stop, study the posted schedule, but clearly decide to use the tube. Bus times on the prison route aren't very frequent on weekends. A few cars drive by sporadically but no other pedestrians are in the vicinity. A bleak wind is probably keeping most folks indoors. Greg is no more than two paces behind the pair as they trudge along, heads down, beside the strangely named Streetwise Knowledge School. They are absorbed in their togetherness, unaware of his proximity.

The leafy trees make a nice canopy overhead, spreading fully across the road, and temporarily darkening the footpath area. As they approach the back gate of the Caledonian Methodist Church, Greg moves forward and swings his right leg with no small force inwards across the woman's ankles. She immediately stumbles, letting go of her companion, and falls to the ground, trying to look behind and yell at her attacker at the same time. Greg knows she'll be immobile for just a few seconds. As Michael turns towards him, Greg delivers a searing uppercut to the man's chin, causing him to buckle and pass out. Greg grabs the woman's handbag and tips its contents all over her, then pulls off both her shoes and throws them high into the tree branches on the other side of the road.

The woman swears loudly, and calls out 'Police, Police, Help!' As she struggles to sit up, Greg steps behind her and quickly duct-tapes her wrists together, then stuffs a rag he's brought along for the purpose in her mouth. He drags her through the church's back gate out of sight of the roadway, then puts a headlock around Michael, who is just coming to. Walking backwards, he drags Michael along the narrow lane behind the school to the parking area at the end of Balmoral Grove. There'd been plenty of parking spaces available when he arrived an hour earlier since none of the businesses lining the street were open on a Saturday afternoon.

Michael puts up a heavy struggle, yelling as he gets his wind back, so Greg stops and hits him hard on the back of his head with a black rubber cosh. Michael goes limp again. It is a tad awkward for Greg to maneuver his well-built victim into the car, but no-one comes by to ask what is going on. It's as if everyone has stayed away from the area on purpose. Greg has his tale ready, however, just in case. His friend is ill, has thrown up, and Greg is planning to take him to the nearest hospital. Could the enquirer tell him how to get there please?

Greg drives away carefully and pulls into an alleyway that runs off Caledonian down near Thornhill Square. There, he gags and trusses Michael up tightly, lays him across the back seat, places a blanket over him, and heads off towards the western outskirts of the city.

***   ***   ***

The following morning, on page two of the Daily Mail there is a small clipping about a man who had been kidnapped the day before in broad daylight. His girlfriend described the attacker as a very large dark-skinned man with straight jet black hair, about age thirty, wearing jeans, a dark blue jacket, and sunglasses. She had no suggestions as to why she and her boyfriend were attacked, and surmised that someone in prison must have arranged the incident. A cleaning lady in an office complex overlooking a nearby parking area said she saw a man dressed similarly about the time of the attack bundle something large into the back seat of a four-door silver sedan car and drive away.

Police are asking for anyone who might have extra information to come forward. There was unofficial speculation by an officer that the victim, whose name was withheld, might have been involved with drugs. If he had taken advantage of inmates while in prison, the kidnapping could be a form of retribution. The investigation is ongoing, he said.

***   ***   ***

Greg dons his thick blue coat, sunglasses, and black hair piece, and drives from the quaint country inn to the isolated farm house where his captive is shackled in a prison-like cell. Fastened to a hook in the center of the floor, the end of one heavy chain clamps around Michael's left ankle, the second chain is tethered similarly to his left wrist. The prisoner has limited movement to a table where food is just in reach and to a toilet at the other end of the cell. A mattress on a metal bed twelve inches off the ground stretches along the back wall.

"Who the fuck are you? What the fuck is going on?" Michael yells. "Ge me out of here. You have no fucking right to hold me. Let me go!"

Greg lets him rant for a few minutes then sits down on the stool by the vertical bars at the front of the cell that surround the entrance door.

"Let's test your memory, Michael," Greg states. "Who is Daniella Montieth?"

No response other than a twitch across Ayoade's face.

"OK, then who is Tasneem Kabir?"

Same twitch.

"Oh, I'm disappointed Michael. Those are the two young women you viciously attacked and punched unconscious four and five years ago. Some of us think four years in jail doesn't nearly make up for the trauma you caused both girls. Did you know your blows broke their teeth, left facial scars that are still evident today and ruined one of Tasneem's eyes? Nasty, vicious punches Michael. Justified by you because you didn't like the way the teenagers looked at you. Incredible, and totally ridiculous bullshit! You are nothing but a scumbag of the first order, just one level above a child abuser. I hope they had fun with you in prison, you foreign piece of shit!

"It's clear you are a racist pig Michael. You stink. You are a bully, a coward, a totally despicable thug. There is no way the population wants you back on the streets again to punch more defenseless women. Are you remembering the girls now? How would you feel if I'd beaten your girlfriend yesterday like you had beaten those two strangers years ago? Not too good I expect.

"Well, I'm not here to lecture you Michael. I just can't stand criminals like you who get too lenient a sentence that allows them to commit more of their crimes afterwards. This is where some of us take the law into our own hands."

Michael's vocal cords get into action again. "Fuck off you bastard. Who the fuck do you think you are? What the fuck is this place? The police will eventually find you and fuck you over man. Undo these chains."

Greg stands up slowly and sneers in his victim's face. "I am the police Michael. At least they wish they could be more like me. Even now I doubt there's much of an effort to find you given all their more-important activities. They think some drug lords have taken you away. At least that's what the papers say this morning.

"But enough of this jawboning. Here's how I view things Michael. For you to punch those girls so viciously that you made them fall to the ground unconscious means you must have a massively strong arm and an amazingly forceful hand. I can think of no reason why those two body parts should remain that way. None at all."

Greg unlocks the door to the cell, picks up a baseball bat stashed beside it and advances towards Michael. As expected, Michael backs up, and lifts his right arm in a defensive gesture as he retreats towards the bed. Greg swings the bat hard into Michael's midsection. The man doubles over, howling in pain, and drops his arm to hold his midriff. Greg raises the bat again and brings it down with all his strength on Michaels' right shoulder. The cracking sound as the humerus bone splits reverberates around the brick walls of the cell. Michael screams and crumples to the floor in agonizing pain. As he drops his manacled left hand to the floor to support himself, Greg delivers a ferocious blow, breaking several fingers.

Michael throws up. His howls diminish as he works on his breathing to avoid choking. As strong as he is, he resorts to whimpering. Greg looks at him in disgust. "Now you have an idea how those girls felt Michael, except you are still conscious. They weren't. Clearly I didn't hit you hard enough. Perhaps this will help."

Greg withdraws the rubber cosh from his waistband and delivers two quick blows, one across Michael's mouth, the other across his right eye. A tooth rattles on the floor and blood drips from both the eye and mouth areas.

Greg retrieves several paper towels and tosses them on the floor. He backs up to the doorway, but calmly says "I'll be back in a minute Michael. Clean yourself up, we have a plane to catch."

He exits the cell and hastens to access a medical kit he has stashed in the next room. He withdraws a syringe and fills it with a colourless liquid from a medical drug container. He returns to the cell and before Michael can react injects him in his upper arm. "Don't worry Michael, that's just a powerful pain-killer that will have you feeling better in no time. Now, get up and let's get out of here."

Amazingly, Michael is able to walk with support after Greg releases him from the chains. He's pushed into the passenger seat of the red rental car Greg hired late last night and the seat-belt is locked into place. Greg turns to his passenger. "I should also tell you that the pain-killer drug allows you very limited muscle movement. Trying anything more than the short walk you just made will be impossible. So, sit back and relax. It's a thirty minute drive to Heathrow at this time of day."

Greg is not one to share his vigilante philosophies with his victims, nor to listen to their rants and raves as they stall for time. He likes to get things over and done with in a hurry, so he can move on. This 'episode', as he likes to think about it, is working out as well as could be hoped.

***   ***   ***

Greg has a number of unwritten rules for his escapades. He responds only to imbecilic public acts, nothing private. He works alone, uses cash in any necessary transactions, and owns a number of fake passports. His only real indulgence is an electronic technology network system in his office that would be the envy of any super computer technician. The sale of his software company years ago created an investment account measured in billions of dollars. The hardest part of the sale was effecting his disappearance over time to become the recluse he is now. Plastic surgery, name changes, relocation, giving up friends, charities, and activities was a long, difficult process, but his reward is his independence and the ability to do exactly what he wants.

The drug in Michael is still active when they reach the airport. Greg leaves the car in long-term parking and takes the shuttle bus to the international terminal 5 from which British Airways flies to Lagos. Check-in is straightforward, although Greg makes sure he speaks for his zombie-like friend, whom he has cleaned up to look reasonably presentable. Greg bought the tickets ahead of time, requiring only Michael's actual passport at check-in. It had been held at the prison for four years and is still valid. Greg uses a fake British passport to secure his booking. The two electronic tickets are validated, and with only two small carry-on bags, the pair take seats in a large lounge reserved for business class passengers. When boarding is announced Greg takes Michael to the men's room and gives him another injection that will keep the pain at bay at least until they land.

Greg knows that Michael is feeling numb. People look at the bandages that were added around his mouth and eye and conclude the man had a nasty fall or has been in a fight. His right arm hangs limp and he keeps his crushed hand hidden in the pocket of his coat. Several times the pair pass by patrolling airport police officers but Michael makes no attempt to communicate with them. A little memory loss drug Greg added to the pain killer medication is working perfectly.

***   ***   ***

It's a long flight to Lagos, and by the time they arrive, Michael's imposed stupor is beginning to fade. As the plane touches down Greg turns to him, and says, "Even the Nigerian community back in London disowned you Michael, so here you are back in your own country. I really doubt you'll ever be granted a visa to go back to the UK, but believe me, if it happens I will know about it and will be waiting for you."

"Fuck you, you bastard," Michael retorts. "I will contact the police the minute I am through customs. You will never get away you fucker. I am a citizen here. I speak the language. You do not, you fucker. You are a dead man."

"I think it might take a while for the authorities here to believe you Michael. You have nothing but the few toiletries I put in your bag, no money, no job, no address. And only a weird story about how some man flew all the way here with you in business class after capturing you and breaking a few bones. I'd deny ever seeing you before boarding. Doesn't make sense. And how did you have enough cash to buy your ticket? If you're lucky they may call a doctor to check you over. You can always hope he won't find the small package of powder sewn into the lining of one of your pants' legs. By the time they poke holes in your story I'll be long gone. Welcome home to HIV land."

Michael turns and screws up his face. "Fuck you, you shit." The passengers are deplaning and he says no more as Greg's words sink in. The pair part company at the immigration stands separating citizens and visitors. Greg wonders if there'll be a scene but it doesn't happen. Michael is through first and turns, giving Greg a hateful stare, then is gone. On clearance, Greg heads for a men's room, removes his glasses, coat and wig, washes the tanning solution off his face, puts on a totally new outfit, and heads to the ticket counters to pick up his return ticket held in a different name.

***   ***   ***

News of Michael Ayoade's disappearance and the ongoing search for him now occupies more space in the tabloids. An enterprising reporter, working backwards from criminal release times at the Pentonville prison, put two and two together to find the name of the man abducted in full daylight. The girlfriend knocked down in the attack has been interviewed, and has revealed how she became acquainted with Michael through online email. She had visited him several times in prison and he had never indicated any concerns about his getting out. He was looking forward to starting a new life and putting the past behind him. The couple had even talked about marriage. She expected to receive a cell phone call anytime now demanding a ransom for her beau's release. The police are skeptical.

Greg buys two copies of the Daily Mail which include a mug shot of Michael. Wearing latex gloves, Greg carefully trims the relevant pages. One of his prized possessions is an old typewriter which he now uses to type a sequence of words along the edge of the photo page, "He is back in Nigeria. You are safe."

Greg places the pages in separate envelopes and addresses them to the two girls who survived Michael's attacks years earlier. He needs no thanks, but takes solace in feeling his actions will make the girls feel more secure when they go out in public in the future.

He relishes the feelings of another job well done. Once more his sense of justice has been served. And he knows, given the weird behaviour patterns of certain individuals at large in the world, that it won't be long before he is able to serve again. Full employment guaranteed!

Michael Ayoade, originally from Nigeria, viciously attacked two single women on separate occasions, for no good reason other than he didn't like the way the women looked at him. The second of these seemingly random acts, which occurred on 13 November 2012, occurred directly in the view of a CCTV camera. The video was shared publicly by police and Ayoade was readily identified and captured. See

http://www.dailymail.co.uk/news/article-2237501/Thug-Michael-Ayoade-36-admits-punching-Tasneem-Kabir-16-unconscious-shocking-random-street-attack.html

On checking further, police found an earlier, similar incident that occurred 20 November 2011.

Ayoade was sentenced to to four years prison by Judge Roger Chaple of the Inner London Crown Court on Monday 25 February 2013.

See
https://www.theguardian.com/uk/2013/feb/25/east-london-man-jailed-attacks

Vancouver Island, Canada, 2017

Table of Contents

Cleaning Up

Chapter 1

I have a hard and fast rule when docking my boat. "Go no faster than the speed at which I want to slam into the concrete pier." The number fixed in my brain is 2 knots. I practice executing my rule religiously. The expense of repairing boats isn't like the cost of repairing cars. Manufacturers don't make a lot of spare parts for boats. If you need one, you pay. Exorbitantly.

There's still a lot of art in making large luxury boats. It isn't an easily reproducible process like that used in creating luxury cars, although the use of robots, which are faster and less expensive, is increasing.

The factory I had visited in Piantedo, Italy was the ultimate in precision component manufacturing. I'd witnessed the robots working on my own 50ft express cruiser there. Incredibly impressive. Cruisers, with their low profile, sleek lines, one or two staterooms, large cockpit lounge and galley are built for speed, not families. Popular, fun boats in our northern waters.

Yet much is still in the hands of artisans and craftsmen whose fathers and grandfathers had worked at the factory. One senses their pride in the smooth gelcoat on the hull, the burnished wood of the helm, and the hand-stitching of the beautiful leather seats. Anything so beautiful, created with pride and love, deserves looking after.

I treasure all the craftsmanship that makes my boat such a pleasure to drive, whether speeding across the water or easing to a stop at a dock. As I move the throttle into neutral and turn off the ignition, I become aware of two uniformed gentlemen and another man waiting twenty feet back in the darkened interior of the mooring shed. I jump down onto the finger dock and tie off fore and aft as the men stroll my way. There doesn't seem to be any urgency in their movements, although I'm curious as to their presence. I wait for them to speak and introduce themselves.

One of the uniformed chaps speaks up.   "Dr. Hoskins? We're from the Anacortes Customs Office. Wonder if we could have a chat?"

"What's this about gents? I' need to wash the salt water off my boat. She likes to be rinsed clean after a run. Can we chat while I hose her down? Helps if I do it before the salt dries."

The trio don't look particularly happy, but nod their heads in agreement. I grab the coiled up hose on the dock, attach it to the faucet, and walk forward to the bow to start my routine. I stop and turn. "May I see your credentials officers?" I ask. They produce authentic looking cards about the size of drivers' licenses, and I quickly scan and return them. The third man is with the police. I turn on the spigot, directing the strong plume of fresh water to the front deck.

"We understand you've been in Desolation Sound Dr. Hoskins. Can you confirm that please?"   I'm surprised. My boat is unique for sure. There are no others like it in the Northwest waters. Someone must have noticed it there and let these folks know. I'd probably spent no more than an hour looking for a spot to anchor in part of the Sound before deciding to move on. Prideaux Haven was too busy for my likes. I disliked the noisy yells of kids having a good time.

I had wanted more peace and quiet, so I headed to Okeover Arm and pulled deep inside Grace Harbour, just a few miles to the south. Found the perfect stern-tie location. No wind, just the gentle noises of nature onshore, a little more algae than I cared for in the water, but I had no intention of swimming. Only two other boats in the vicinity. Near perfect!

While my mind wondered where this conversation might lead, I answered the officer's question "Yes, sir, although I wasn't there for very long."

"Did you notice anything unusual, sir, while you were there?"

"Like what, sir?" I re-direct the hose to the starboard hull.

"People, or boats behaving strangely, unusual activity on shore, that sort of thing."

"No. The only thing that caught my attention was a seaplane landing just off the Paige Islets as I was leaving."

"When was that, sir?"

The men are friendly and polite but I am getting a bit annoyed that they aren't sharing anything with me. Why are they interviewing me? What is going on?

"Must have been Tuesday sometime just after lunch. I wasn't keeping close track of time. Why am I being questioned?"

"It's about a missing person, sir, which is why Detective Robertson is with us. You didn't check in at Roche Harbor on your return trip so we thought we'd catch up personally."

This still wasn't making any sense. I turn off the hose. "I called the 800 number as I motored across Haro Strait, gave my clearance code, and was approved to come directly back to Anacortes. I've done that many times. You can check the record I'm sure."

There was something they weren't telling me. Damn them! I needed to finish washing down my boat and go home. I turn the water back on, walk around to the port side and hose the hull there. They follow me. A Customs chap asks, "Do you have a zodiac sir? We didn't see you bring one in."

Good God, these are supposedly the 'water police' of Homeland Security. Clearly they are not mature boaters. And/or they aren't looking too closely at my vessel. I am getting more and more peeved.

I'm conscious of the need to be civil in my response, but I fail. All I can come out with is "Do you keep your personal car in a garage at home officer. Or do you leave it out on the street overnight? We all need a zodiac, to get to shore or reach other boats. You see all the boats in the marina here? Do you see their zodiacs? Some on the fore deck, some on the roof, some hinged behind, and a few in the water at the stern or bow. Now where's mine? Gee, maybe this boat has a garage. Is that possible? Why yes, lookie there. Could the zodiac be inside? Let's take a look shall we?"

In order to help myself calm down and perhaps irritate the officers, I turn off the hose and wind it with slow, deliberate motion into a series of rising concentric circles, and place it out of the way on the concrete dock.

I step back onboard, reach up inside the rear salon and press the switch which raises the roof of my 10 foot garage.

There, in all its glory, sits my little runabout zodiac.

And within it, in somewhat less glory, lies the nude body of a young woman, twisted in a position that is far from normal.

Chapter 2

I'm sitting in the local police station wondering how much longer I'll have to wait around. I've been here for three hours and the fuzz aren't finished with me yet. Different detectives have been taking turns grilling me. Detective Robertson, whom I met earlier, pushes open the door to my interrogation room, replacing one of his associates. I remark his ill-fitting jacket, small dobs of cigarette ash evident in a couple of places.

Robertson speaks up. "Dr. Hoskins, let's go over things one more time."

I'm losing count of how many times I've answered similarly-phrased questions from different officers. I decide to take the initiative anyway as an attempt to relieve the routine.

"So, is she the 'missing person' you alluded to down at the dock?"

"It's possible she is indeed the 'Jane Doe' missing from Campbell River on Vancouver Island. You've never seen her before?"

I shake my head. "I haven't been in Campbell River in years."

"Still, I need to go over your trip details one more time to see if we can work out how her body got in your garage."

I cringe at the thought of having to repeat myself. Robertson continues, fixing small steely eyes on me.

"Let me see if I have things straight. Outbound, after leaving Sidney you spent a few days anchoring out in the Broughton Archipelago then stayed overnight at Blind Channel on your way back. After that you wnet to nearby Dent Island Resort where you did some salmon fishing. Stayed there three days. That shouldn't be hard to check. Pretty cooperative folks up there."

I nod my head, "Correct. From the harbor-master to the chef, to the fishing guides, and management, it's a first-class resort. I go back at least every two years."

"Why? Tell me more."

"The place has a fabulous location in the middle of pristine wilderness. Fierce rapids in the surrounding waterways make the timing of access crucial. Captains don't pull in there on a whim. Safe docking is always a relief. And it's not a place where families go for fun. I like the quiet seclusion."

"You've said you didn't use your runabout while there. Makes sense if you went out with the local guides. After your stay you then headed back south and checked out Prideaux Haven, but decided not to anchor there. Tell us about the seaplane you said you saw landing near there."

I close my eyes and work on recall. "It was one of the smaller planes owned by Kenmore Air down on Lake Washington in Seattle. I've seen bunches of them over the years, even taken flights in them.

"First time I'd seen one of their planes land in open water like that, however. I mean, usually when I see them, they are flying people to a resort or town. Friday Harbor, Dent Island Resort, etc. I presumed this must have been a charter, not one of their regularly scheduled flights. I was surprised by the number of zodiacs around the plane. Must have been six. It just struck me as odd unless a bunch of people were getting off the plane. I didn't stay to check further."

Robertson asks, "Did you get any impression that someone was boarding the plane as opposed to getting off, by any chance?"

I sit upright. The question has triggered further recall.

"Funny you mention that.   I glimpsed someone on a stretcher at the passenger door. Whether they were being loaded or unloaded I couldn't say. A number of people were standing in their inflatables, some hanging on to the float struts. Now that you ask, I remember thinking at the time that perhaps it was an invalid coming to spend a few days with friends on the water, someone who couldn't tolerate turbulent crossings of the Strait of Georgia and Malaspina Strait. Guess I forgot about it pretty quickly."

"OK, so after leaving there you anchored in Grace Harbor. You must have used the dinghy to stern tie to trees on shore. Right?"

Robertson clearly had some experience out on the water.

"For sure."

"And that's the last time you used the runabout? After that you felt it was safely locked away in the garage?"

"Ah, not quite."

"What do you mean? That's what you indicated earlier." The detective leans forward, anticipation written across his jowls.

"I forgot something. The night before I left Grace Harbor I used the runabout to go five miles south down Okeover Arm and have dinner at the Laughing Oyster restaurant in Lund. Love their food. I had a reservation and they'll confirm I was there. I didn't put the dinghy back in the garage until the next morning before leaving."

I wring my hands together, feeling bad that I hadn't remembered that jaunt previously.   I don't want any suspicion cast on me.

The second officer in the room weighs in. "And from Grace Harbour you went directly back to the Port of Sidney Marina, where you stayed two nights?"

"Yes. That must be where the woman was put in the garage. I never used the inflatable there. And I think I know when she was dumped in it. By the way, from what I saw before you hustled me away, I'm sure that woman wasn't murdered on my boat based on the skin sheen and the discolored patches., I've seen many dead bodies during my career."

"What else?"

"Well, I guess from the quick glance I got at the marks around her throat that she'd been strangled. I bet she was killed somewhere else and then brought to the marina and stowed in my boat."

"How would that be possible without being seen? Seems very unlikely."

"It must have been done at night, probably early morning when everyone was sleeping. The only way one can get into the docks from the street after the marina closes is with a gate card. Those are provided when the boat is registered with the marina office. So whoever did this, they must have been off a boat in the marina. They must have seen my garage open at some point during the day."

Here I go playing detective. 'Way to go', I tell myself!

'How about letting the experts work?'

"Hold up a minute Dr. Hoskins. I'm not buying this. Opening and closing your garage is noisy. Surely the sound would have woken you if you were aboard. And wouldn't someone need to know where the control button was? Now, were you aboard, or were you staying elsewhere that night?"

"Sounds like you all think I'm a suspect, Detective." I want this conversation to be over, so I swallow my rising anger and respond calmly.

"On the afternoon after my arrival at the marina I opened the waterproof container in the front of the dinghy to retrieve a copy of the menu I'd taken with me from the Laughing Oyster. I wanted to check the name of the appetizer dish I'd had there. There was no body present in the garage, that's for sure."

Robertson interrupts. "OK, OK. Move on."

He's testy. I'm getting pissed-off again, but contain my anger. "I stayed up, reading late into the night."

"What book?"

"Probably one you'd never choose to read, Detective. It's a popular book about nautical war escapades in 1800s Europe called 'Master and Commander' by Patrick O'Brian. Did you not see it on the bookshelf by my bed in the boat?"

"Get on with it Hoskins."

"Yes sir, certainly sir."

"The next night I had dinner at the Deep Cove Chalet restaurant up on the north end of the Saanich Peninsula. I drank far more than usual – a beautiful French Montrachet that was hard to put down. Thank heavens I took a taxi each way and didn't rent a car. Back in the boat I must have really zonked out, because I was still a bit foggy the next morning. I never heard anything that night, such as the garage opening and closing. Although the murderer wouldn't have needed to open it fully."

"A bit coincidental Hoskins. The murderer just happens to be in your marina. Sees you come home late, somewhat inebriated. Knows how to open your garage. And drags a body into your zodiac without you hearing anything. Is that what you are trying to sell me?"

"That must be how it was, Detective."

"Ok Hoskins. You can go, but your boat is off-limits tonight and tomorrow. Should be available day after next unless there are other developments. No more excursions into Canadian waters until I contact you. Make sure we know where to find you."

I leave hurriedly, glad to be released. They probably would have been within their rights to hold me in a cell overnight. But somewhere, deep in my brain, a thought nags at me as I walk along the waterfront. I replay the interrogations with Robertson and his associates over and over, trying to identify my concern. The wind whips at my hair and clothes, adding to my irritation. Finally, I decide to let it go for now and to re-try in the morning.

And, as is often the case when the mind is freed, the hidden concern immediately bubbles to the surface.

Why hadn't they asked me the one specific question I would have dreaded?

Chapter 3

I manage to eat a light breakfast and on arriving back at the marina am not surprised to find yellow tape blocking access to the ramp where my boat is moored. A police officer challenges me, but lets me proceed when I tell him who I am and which boat I own.

There are a number of technicians in white protective suits swarming throughout the berth. Beside the boat, on the boat, and probably deep inside the boat. I'd given the police my duplicate set of ignition keys last night. They'd moved the cruiser forward so the inflatable could be winched out and placed in the water behind. The woman's body had been moved from the garage but there was a black zipped body bag lying on the main walkway, waiting to be picked up.

Detective Robertson hops off the boat and walks up to me. He holds a large clear plastic bag with red material in it. He lifts it up before my eyes. He isn't smiling.

"We found this stuffed into a crevice behind one of the closet drawers in the main salon. Recognize it?"

His voice is stern and I suddenly realize he thinks it could belong to the murdered woman and that I had hidden it.

I look more closely at the bag's contents. Inside is a bunched-up scarf, plain red, of thin material. I see a couple of long hairs tangled in one corner and breathe a sigh of relief. I reply calmly, "Yes, I recognize it, Detective. That belonged to my wife who died a year ago. I tried to remove everything of hers from the boat after she passed. Thought I'd done a pretty good job. I wonder how I missed this. Did you find anything else?"

"We did." Semi-triumphant tone.

"Recovered blonde hairs from your rear bathroom."

The dead woman was a blonde.

The cops have obviously been very thorough checking the boat. Their invasiveness irritates me. Am I becoming a suspect rather than just a person of interest? I wait for the obvious question, but get a surprise.

"Was your wife blonde?" The way Robertson asks the question bothers me. His tone taunts, his tiny eyes mere slits. Clearly the police are checking whether the dead woman had been elsewhere on the boat other than the garage. I give them credit for good detective procedure, since the latter 'hair' find naturally raises suspicions. If I answer 'No', life will undoubtedly get awkward.

"That requires more than a simple response, Detective."

"Then get on with it, Hoskins."

"My wife was a natural blonde, but in the last years of her life, she colored her hair a light reddish color."

Robertson's face morphs to a hint of smugness. "The hairs from the drain are pubic hairs, not crown hairs. We'll analyze them. I need something personal of your wife's to check the DNA."

His tone has become more formal. He hopes for no match.

Prick!

Once again I summon up control. "I don't have a hairbrush or toothbrush, Detective. And I disposed of all her make-up items and underwear, and gave all her good clothes to charity. Won't those hairs caught in the scarf be sufficient?"

Robertson pauses, assessing my believability.

His eyes never leave mine. After 20 seconds his bearing changes.

Agreement.

My answers have kept me out of jail, although I'm not a free man yet.

 "No point hanging around here, Hoskins. We have work to do. We should be able to release your boat tomorrow if there are no significant findings. Call me at the office in the morning to check."

With that, the man turns and walks away.

For the moment, I am not about to be arrested for a crime I didn't commit.

 Of course the police have no idea about the crime I did commit.

I hope to keep it that way.

Chapter 4

I pull the pre-paid cellphone from my jacket pocket and dial long distance. The call is answered at the first ring.

"Hi Derwent. Been wondering when you'd call."

"What the fuck were you thinking, Graham? The cops found the girl you killed and stuck in my garage when I docked. Thanks to you they're all over me and now my boat is quarantined. Why the Hell did you break the rules? We agreed we wouldn't cruise anywhere near each other on the water. Too risky. What the fuck, man?"

"Calm down Derwent. How come the cops found her? And don't yell at me about rules. Prideaux Haven was my turf. You poked your nose in at the wrong time. You knew I was in the Campbell River and Desolation Sound area. You shouldn't have been anywhere close. I saw you by the seaplane."

"Yeah, Graham, right. That was sheer coincidence. Is that why you dumped the blonde girl in my boat, to get even?"

"No way. Listen. The kid being loaded into the seaplane got off lightly. He'd been terrorizing swimmers and boaters with his expensive PWC, racing around the bay at high speed. He nearly ran over a young girl as she jumped off a pontoon. He crashed on shore into the rocks. Broke both legs, his pelvis, and his back when his fuel tank developed a leak, and emptied out, courtesy my handiwork. Rich Daddy must have charted the float plane – probably sent him off to Harborview hospital down in Seattle."

"Forget the damn kid, Graham. I could care less. You still haven't told me why you dumped the girl in my boat. What the fuck for? Bloody damned stupid in my view. What made you stick her on me? You've probably caused me no end of future trouble. I'm lucky I'm not calling you from a jail cell."

"Look, Derwent, it was like this. You'd dgotten rid of your two victims up in bear country near Blind Channel. I left my first one up in the Octopus Islands. I just thought it wouldn't be smart to have them all dropped in Canada, at the same time. Maybe one in the U.S. would spread the risk. I don't have U.S. clearance so I made a speedy run to get her on your boat. I didn't want to use our phones in case the call could be intercepted, and I didn't want to wake you. No way I could have predicted authorities would be there when you pulled in. That's just freakish bad luck!"

"I don't agree with your thinking. Why not just wait a couple of days instead of involving me? Dumb, Graham, dumb. Too much could go wrong, and it has. Shit, fuck. I'm the one who'll pay the consequences of your stupidity, dammit!"

Silence on the other end.

I continue.

"We need to meet in person and chat this through. Sooner the better. Nanaimo next Thursday? Usual place and time and I'll bring two new phones."

"Ok, Derwent. I'm sorry for the hassle. I never guessed you'd get intercepted. The only good part is that several more prostitutes and a pimp are permanently out of work. And one shitass kid put on ice for a while   See you Thursday."

I hang up, still fuming. Teeth grinding. Damn, damn, damn.

As I cross the slough on the road out of town, I hurl the burner phone into its slimy depths. Good riddance.

Now, how the heck do Graham and I resolve things?

Chapter 5

The phone rings insistently. It is early for a call – 7:23 am by my bedside clock. I suppress a yawn and mumble, "Hello?"

"Dr. Hoskins? Detective Robertson. We're finished with your boat, but we have more questions."

I try to be affable, despite my haziness, as this is a pleasant surprise. I'm addressed as 'Dr. Hoskins', not just 'Hoskins'. Not like yesterday morning.

"It's early, but thanks for letting me know. Can we discuss the questions later? I'm not really awake yet."

"Will you be back in Anacortes in the next few days? If so we could hold off till then."   Mellow tone, which makes me suspicious.

"I'll be there early Thursday. Would that work?"

"Sure, come by the office any-time after 8 am. See you then."

As I'd indicated to Graham, I'm not free yet.   Damn Graham. Damn the detective. Damn the dead woman.

What the hell does Robertson want now? Couldn't be too urgent or he'd want to see me immediately. And I think everything should be over with the release of the boat. But apparently not. In my mind, I've been debating whether to buy a replacement zodiac, although the current one has seen far worse than that dead woman.   It's a pain to get another zodiac exactly the same size to fit the foreign-designed cruiser garage, so I'm tempted to leave things as they are.

I'm not happy about having to answer more police questions. Will they be a prelude to another interrogation? I gnaw my lip.

On Thursday morning when we greet, Detective Robertson smiles. Big smiles early in the morning are flashing neon warning signals in my book, especially on someone with little steely eyes. False cheer meant to distract. I don't trust him. He asks where I'm headed, and fidgets. Can hardly wait for me to complete my answers before he's on to his next barrage. The smile has disappeared. I tell him Nanaimo.

"Do you always travel alone, Doctor?"

"Like I told you yesterday, my wife died nearly a year ago, so no one helps me pilot the boat now."

"Yes, but surely you have guests from time to time, right?" He is getting close to some   sensitive issues. My nerves twitch. I work hard to project an aura of calm.

"Well, there's always guests at marinas who want to look over the boat and learn more about it. As I told you before, there's no cruiser like it in these parts."

"So you have women onboard?"

My brain flashes a danger signal. I quickly dismiss a thought of whether the questions would be different if a male had been discovered in the boat's garage. I concentrate on keeping my cool.

"Of course I have women onboard. It's easy to become friendly with other captains and crews at the marinas. Many are husbands and wives out together. We often sit and have drinks on the docks or on our rear decks and salons. We share experiences, information on marinas, waterways, the currents, weather conditions, anchorage spots, and our boats. In remote areas, it's standard social behavior. What's this all about, Detective?"

Here it comes. The friendly upfront demeanor is about to morph into something ominous. "A dockhand at the Dent resort says he saw a young woman stepping off your boat very early one morning and running along the dock to another boat moored nearby. She was skimpily dressed and in a hurry."

Damn. I need to stall while I think. I try a non-sequitur. "Was she breaking the law, or is there some particular interest you have in this woman, Detective?"

"From the description the dockhand gave I wondered if she's the woman we found in your boat."

"You're still trying to link me to the dead woman from Campbell River? I'll repeat myself, Detective. I never saw her before anywhere, anytime, until we opened the boat garage. Who the heck is she? Have you found that out yet? Why do you think I have a relationship with the poor woman? Do you really think I'd have opened the garage if I knew I'd put her there? Someone else dumped her on my boat. I'm sure you checked the Campbell River Marina records and found the last time I was in that town was 18 months ago."

As I speak, I'm cursing Graham in my mind.

"You aren't denying the dockhand's story, Hoskins. Presumably, the female he saw was onboard your boat overnight then? A friend, or something a little more daring? A call girl, perhaps?"

The tone is sinister again. From his semi-friendly phone call, I had expected less pointed questions. I resent the suggestions he's making and the accompanying sneer. With good reason. I hesitate, working to keep my anger in check, run my fingers through my hair, think of Graham again, and swallow noisily.

"Why would I avoid responding to the dockhand's input? I'm just pissed at your suspicious mind, Detective. That morning, Mrs. Jenkins popped along the dock from her boat in quite a dither. Said her husband was having chest pains. Asked if I would check him out. She ran back, and I followed a minute later after retrieving my medical bag from the front salon. Was nothing more than severe indigestion."

Robertson looks deflated. I continue. "I'm sure Mrs. Jenkins will corroborate my story. I believe the Jenkins' home port is in Vancouver somewhere. You can get contact information from the folks at Dent Island."

I stare belligerently into Robertson's eyes. He's gotten way under my skin. I've had enough. He says nothing.

"If you have no more silly doubts to explore now, I'll be on my way to Nanaimo."

I can't resist a parting jab.

"If I were you, I'd work closely with the Canadian authorities to learn more about that poor girl. Whoever filed that missing person's report should come down here and see if he or she can help with identification."

I turn and leave. I don't need more prying questions. They might just luck onto one that causes difficulties. If I have to, I'll lie. Done it many times, but I've found it's better, if I can, to avoid the need, and so I try to say as little as possible.

Unless I'm being asked annoying questions by utter boors.

Robertson is getting too close.

Chapter 6

After leaving the police station I stop for coffee and decide to mentally retrace the steps that led me into Robertson's clutches. I certainly never intended to arrive home with a dead body on board. I start with the memory of driving late at night along narrow streets a few blocks from the center of a small coastal town. Turning onto a better lit thoroughfare I spy a number of whores near a corner.

I pull up and eagerly watch one of the gals sashay onto the roadway as I let down the curbside window. A big frizzy hairdo adds inches to her natural height and makes her short skirt look even skimpier. It's a bright silver color, like her blouse, providing a vivid contrast with her dark brown skin.

"Lookin' for some fun, mister?" she coos leaning into the car, jostling her large silicon-enhanced boobs in practiced fashion. They're well exposed and very attractive but I resist the temptation to fondle them.

"Yeah," I say, "$200 for an hour, my place."

"$400," she counters, "And you show me cash now."

"$300 and that's tops, love." I show her a fanned-out fistful of 50 dollar bills.

She opens the passenger door and plunks way down in the seat. "I'm Carla. Where we going, Sugar?" she croons.

"Waterfront," is all I say.

"Ooh, I like waterbeds. Nice and bouncy. Puts some fun in the old 'dip-it-in' routine." Dumb woman, high on some drug, I don't care which one. She won't need any more after tonight, so it doesn't matter.

The only light on at the marina is over the office door, shining down on the metal grill covering the top concrete step. Resident boaters and visitors are advised by multiple posted signs to always carry a flashlight at night. Much cheaper for the marina owners than floodlights all over the place, I guess.

The gal has trouble negotiating the wooden planks of the walkways in her high heels, so I tell her to carry her shoes in one hand and walk barefoot, which she does. It isn't far and the wood has been worn smooth over time so there's no fear of splinters. We turn onto my dock and pass two finger piers where the pungent scent of sleeping harbor seals rents the air. She wiggles her ass as she walks ahead of me to the boat I point out, and I help her down into the cockpit area, shining my torch on the narrow steps.

"You used a head before, Miss?" I ask. She nods 'yes' as we

climb down three steps into the main cabin where I switch on the low wattage overhead light. She's serviced lonely sailors overnighting at the marina before.

What I really want is get ahold of her pimp, for pimps are the real pigs. But she's a purveyor and street sex-priestess in her own right, so she counts. I saw her handler on one of my reconnaissance missions, and then at a distance under dim street lights. He'll keep for another time.

She exits the bathroom and immediately demands payment. I hand her the cash which she stuffs in a shoe she's thrown on the floor. She grabs the hem of her low-cut top and reaches up, pulling it slowly up and over her gorgeous boobs and massive crop of hair.

I drive my syringe into a vein in her neck.

She yells "What the fuck?"

Disbelief registers in her eyes which bulge horribly as she staggers backward, stumbling against the bathroom door. She froths at the lips as her face spasms into harsh lines. Pee flows and stains her tight pants. Unconsciousness claims her, and with my help, she crumples to the floor. 25 seconds. I'm getting better at this. Rolling her on her back I administer the lethal cocktail into a vein inside her elbow. I've experimented with various drug mixtures over the years and the current combination is my most reliable.

The girl has no understanding of what hit her, which I believe is a blessing. No lingering. I'm not interested in telling her why she's dying, even if she could hear me, just in getting her to that point quickly. My son's horrible AIDS death, derived from the HIV passed on by an infected prostitute on the other side of the coutry, is avenged again.

It doesn't assuage the pain of his absence however.

I turn out the light, pull on a pair of nylon medical gloves, grab a towel from the head, and carefully and methodically wipe down every surface she might have touched.

I move her to the floor of the main cabin and lay her on a blanket I'd bought on clearance for the occasion. I retrieve my cash from her shoe and can't resist checking inside her purse. No ID of course, but $320 in twenties, a pack of gum, a small vial of cheap perfume, and two packets of condoms. I leave all the contents undisturbed and throw the towel on top of her.

I debate with my alter ego whether to go back and try to pick up her pimp as well. That would be a far more difficult and risky exercise.

I lean towards doing nothing when a totally unexpected deluge of rain suddenly creates a shattering din on the tin roof of the marina.

An omen. Both good and bad.

Chapter 7

I love working in the rain. Heavy squalls keep innocents, and their prying eyes, indoors. Hookers huddle in doorways or under awnings, and pimps often stand with them as business slows down. The transactions that do take place are executed faster than normally. No one wants to get too wet.

I find the keys to the second car I'd stolen early this morning, and retrace my route to the pick-up neighbourhood. My target pimp harangues his girls as they shiver and wait for clients to come by. Rain falls steadily on the canvas awning they huddle under. Boss man raises his fist to one of the girls but she smartly backs off whatever she was mouthing and he desists. Nasty piece of shit. This guy uses his fists to intimidate members of his little harem. He has a broad chest and powerful arms with bulging biceps under his shirt sleeves. Plus, a cocky swagger.

How to catch this creep? As I watch through my binoculars, one of the girls slips as she steps onto the wet sidewalk, goes down hard on her butt, slips further and ends up lying flat on her back. Her friends pull her under cover, but she's given me an idea. I'll use Carla, the dead girl lying prone in my boat, as bait.

I head for the intersection at higher than usual speed. Pull up, spraying water, lower my window, and yell. "Anyone a friend of Carla's? She's sick, needs help." The girls look at each other, and shrug, feigning ignorance. Perhaps because they are unsure of me or more likely because their pimp is present. He saunters towards the car through the pouring rain.

"What you want, motherfucker?" Menacing tone. Dead eyes.

I decide to play the heavy. "Fuck off, shithead, unless you know Carla. She needs to get to a doctor or hospital." I put the car in gear and start to inch away.

"Hold it fucker. Where is she? I look after her sometimes."

"At my place, three minutes from here. She can't stand, her breathing is raspy, no color in her face. Lips turning blue. Get in, I'll take you."

"I'll follow you in my car. Lead on bro'."

"She could die by the time you go get your wheels, big guy. I ain't waitin'. I gotta get back to her. Get in.''

He hesitates. "You fuck with me and you're dead, man." Points to a pistol shape in the pocket of his jacket. Opens the car door.

I move off before he's totally in and the door has closed. Get to the marina in record time. I run ahead to the dock, and notice he has trouble keeping up. Good. He may look athletic but his movements indicate poor fitness. I jump on my boat, run to the locked cabin entryway.   Fumble getting the keys out of my pocket. The pimp is annoyed and suspicious.

"Quit stalling fucker. Where is she?"

The keys drop out of my coat at his feet. He grabs them and muscles me out of the way.

"The blue one on a chain." I tell him.

Perfect. He opens the door, a nd even though the overhead light isn't on, it isn't hard to recognize the ourline of the girl on the rug, and to smell body fluids.

He starts to descend the four steps into the cabin. With one hand I jam two of my syringes into the tight flesh of the left thigh on his back leg. He swears loudly and turns to reach for me. But with my other hand I give him a violent push. His head thuds against the bottom step, and he is out. I wait just under a minute to be sure he'll stay unconscious from my medicine. Vomit spews from his mouth and dribbles onto the girl's blouse. He pees in his pants.

I hate cleaning up after involuntary voiding. Disgusting.

I'll have to see if there is a modification of my poison cocktail that can avoid that.

I administer the coup de grace with a needle into a neck vein. I smile, pleased that the bum was easier to deal with than I expected, and that he's dead.

I lock the boat, and drive to a supermarket parking lot about two miles away. I leave the car there in case any of the girls on the cornermight remember a license plate number. Takes me 30 minutes to walk back to the marina. At least the rain is only a light drizzle and I'm not fighting heavy showers. I throw the car keys in a dumpster behind a shed belonging to a fishing company. Not many folks will want to scour the smelly mess in that bin.

Two in one night. I can't help but smile. I've always been an overachiever.

Chapter 8

Over a leisurely bacon and eggs breakfast at a local café I mentally review a trip I made several years earlier along Johnstone Strait to the Broughton Archipelago, north of

Vancouver Island. After a couple of days meandering the back waterways of this pristine wilderness, I happened upon a small cove with three mooring balls. In the middle of nowhere. Who had put the balls there and why, I wondered? Was it a lumber firm from first growth logging times, or a wildlife service of some entity from much later? I remember the distinctive orange color that made the buoys stand out in the inky back water. The bay was surrounded by large overhanging trees. An ancient First Nation midden loomed at the head of the cove.

Finding that secluded spot was a prize in itself. I tied up to the ball farthest from shore and enjoyed the solitude and privacy of the place. Slept peacefully. In the morning, I woke early to the sound of birds calling. I sauntered upstairs to the rear deck and watched a pair of herons fly over. Turning towards shore, another sight thrilled me. Two black bears ambled down to the midden to snag fish stranded by the low tide that had occurred during the night. They didn't find anything and quietly retreated into the forest.

Based on the resurgence of these memories, I now know the perfect target spot for disposing the two bodies currently polluting my cabin floor. There's a sense of accomplishment when I end a prostitute's career. Double kudos when I rid the streets of a pimp as well. Although, frankly, I fear some of the pimps' girls may have a hard time looking after themselves in their man's absence. Most will probably gravitate to another boss.

I cling to the hope that perhaps at least one ho somewhere has found a better way of life because I've rid her of a domineering male controlling her sorry life.

I'll never know.

What I really wish is that I could stop prostitution in a major city, but that is out of the question. Police records are filled with finds of prostitutes' bodies dumped in abandoned lots, woods, and buildings. Other people clearly feel and act the same way as I do. My efforts at the moment are directed to the little towns along the inside coast of Vancouver Island. It's an area where one man can have an impact, albeit a small one. There are bands of prostitutes there, some of whom ply their trade in the playground towns and waters of Desolation Sound and beyond. Those are the ones that really irk me. They don't all need to die by my hand. If some were to leave their 'profession' that would mean less who could infect future 'Johns'. I do what I can, hoping to scare the ones left behind with the disappearances and deaths of friends and associates.

The morning after my late night efforts with Carla and her pimp, I fill the fuel tanks and head off on the relatively short northwesterly haul up Johnstone Strait, leading into unspoiled Canadian forest country. It is a gorgeous morning, the rain gone, and for a change there is hardly any wind. I take it as a good sign for what I am doing. For sheer pleasure, just as I did last time, I weave in and out of the deep, still passages in the area. Other boats are out and about, the sailboats all running on power given the lack of wind.

I find my semi-hidden cove, and, as suspected, the mooring balls are vacant. I connect to the one nearest to shore this time. Any overnighters that might have been here have already left and it's far too early for those needing an end-of-day anchorage.

I winch the inflatable halfway out of the garage. It's hard work maneuvering the two bodies into it and I'm sweating when done. It only takes a few minutes to slide the tender into the water and row to the midden, however. No way I will land without checking for bears.

I stick two fingers in my mouth and whistle loudly enough to be heard on the other side of the sound to let any hidden beasts know that I'm present. I also yell through my portable hailer and then wait a couple of minutes.Satisfied the nearby woods are empty, I drag the bodies one by one fifty yards beyond the tree-line. Using a downed tree limb, I brush out the tracks, and rub my feet across the marks left in the midden shells.

The bears or wolves will find the couple before any humans do.

The creeps are getting what they deserve.

Chapter 9

This is my last trip in these beautiful northwest islands pursuing vile sex purveyors. No matter how careful I am, it only takes one microscopic blood stain, one nosy marina neighbor, one brilliant cop, and I could be behind bars for the rest of my life, best case. Better to get out now, recognize the revenge achieved, and celebrate my service to humanity with the wind in my face and the sun on my back. Plus, my acquaintance, Graham, has proven unreliable, adding more risk. Smarter if we go separate ways

Through a series of casual meet-ups over the last two years, Graham and I eventually found each other, learning that we had common interests.   It was reassuring to know I wasn't alone in my quest.   The two of us became careful accomplices, nothing more. We shared our names, but not addresses. I live in the U.S., Graham lives in Canada.

I actually suspect the name he gave me is false.

Just like the one I gave him.

I know from newspaper reports that some of the bodies found in Canada correspond with the times and locations he's shared with me after completing his work. We've only met four times, as we communicate primarily via burner phones. Our brief semi-coded conversations indicate where we'll work next, or relate our latest individual venture and result. I'm proud of him when I read an article that chronicles his work. We are both accomplishing good things for society.

However, not only is this my last trip, I'm also bowing out of my fellow vigilante's life. I may continue my work elsewhere at a later date, but for the next few days I'll visit some of my favorite places between this cove and Anacortes before skedaddling.   I'll arrange one last meeting with my partner-in-crime, then I'll disappear. I'll sell the boat, change offices, get rid of the disguises I always work in, and start a new campaign of responding to evil public acts that get ridiculous or no responses. The choices are endless.

Having dumped the two bodies well beyond the midden, I set a course for Blind Channel marina on West Thurlow Island, a small outstation run by a German family which serves wonderful meals in their little restaurant. They offer rustic accommodation, but that is secondary to the marina, water taxi, and restaurant functions.   Behind the scenes there's a lot of fascinating history covering every way of life in the area, from logging to bootlegging to hunting and fishing.

I set off on the track starting behind the restaurant. Weak sunlight filters gently through the shady giant firs, hemlocks, and cedar trees, some nearly 1000 years old, having survived the loggers long ago. The only noise arises from a clear-water brook as it bubbles downhill beside the crushed pine bark path. The pristine temperate rainforest stretches across the island, and there are no serious predators in residence. The lovely, tranquil environment soothes my angry soul.

I stay the night and head off to Dent Island next morning. I plan to moor there a couple of days and nights, after which I will mosey southwards through Desolation Sound, on to Sidney marina, then cross the border and head back to Anacortes.

I'm sure it will feel good to be back home again.

Chapter 10

That was then. The homecoming was anything but good. A surprise welcoming committee at the dock found the dead woman in my boat. Three days later I'm still being questioned, although I'm completely innocent. In this case. How ironic.

Now, with the police station visit behind me, my reminiscence complete, I sit in the coffee shop and order a third cup. I review the just-completed exchange with Robertson. The bitter drink fuels my introspection which makes me even more committed to end my current crusade. Robertson's doggedness, versus brains, could lead him to the solution. Even half-wits get lucky now and then. I'm wary of underestimating what he could discover.

Buoyed by the decision to end my efforts, I walk with vigor to the marina and prepare the boat to head northwest. I look forward to seeing Graham again to discuss things, even though I've made the trip to Nanaimo twenty or more times.

I cross that invisible line in the water that denotes the U.S./Canadian border and head for slack water at Dodd Narrows. I've been to the Nanaimo Port Authority marina often so the narrow waterways pose no problem. I dock at one of the busy piers.

To kill time I take the little ferry to Protection Island, and wander to Blackbeard Park where I sit and watch boats further out at the edge of Georgia Strait. It'll be a long time before I join them again, if ever.

I catch up on the world's news, courtesy of my laptop and a cellular service, and take the jitney ferry back to the marina. I dump the laptop on my boat, pick up some odds and ends and walk to the uptown restaurant where Graham and I always meet.

It's a nondescript place, offering Italian food, completely unexceptional. We meet at 5:30 pm to get a table that allows us to have a discreet conversation not overheard by nearby neighbors. Graham is already there munching on crusty bread, with oil and vinegar for dipping. An open, but un-poured, bottle of Chianti, sits on the table.

There's an air of nervousness clinging to Graham, but we shake

hands firmly and he points to the bottle, looks me in the eye and says, "Thought this might be part of an apology for the trouble I caused you, partner. Dinner is on me as well tonight. Things didn't work out as I'd planned. I feel bad."

My feelings lighten a little.

"I'm still dodging cops, Graham. A detective in Anacortes doesn't buy my story, for whatever reason. I doubt he's had a dead body on a boat before. He's like a terrier that won't give up the bone he's found. I worry he'll stumble onto something that will cause us both problems. Scary, frankly."

"You don't think he'd appreciate the work we are doing for his kindred? In my view, society is better off with our efforts at preventing moral decay."

I gave him a look and he lowers his voice.

Yeah, I think. But are we two better off for those efforts?

At that moment a petite young waitress bounces up to the table. We cease our chat as she parks her gum in one cheek, introduces herself as Gina, and confides, "The lamb shank is great tonight, guys. Grandma's recipe handed down to my Dad. Cooked in red wine to match your Chianti. Trust me, it's terrific. Served with fresh asparagus, fingerling potatoes, and baby carrots. Any interest?"

Clearly, a well-practiced sales pitch. I sincerely doubt the recipe is a family heirloom, but, so what? I'm hungry, and it sounds ideal. Graham wants the veal dish. He's had it before and wasn't at all complimentary, so I'm surprised he wants it again. I ask, "Are you sure? Didn't think it worked for you last time."

"Well, lamb isn't my thing. Maybe the veal will be better this time around." Not for me to argue.

We each toss down a glass of Chianti and I resume my speech. "I'm being given a signal, Graham. We've been very successful in cleaning up certain activities over the years. And we're still scot free. But I'm not prepared to risk any more disposals. I'm glad we're having this meal to celebrate, but I hope you understand I won't be back across the border anymore."

Graham rocks back in his chair. He studies me intensely, puts down his glass, leans across the table. "Really, Derwent? I thought you were the ice-man. Never worried about getting caught with all your preparations. I'm surprised and disappointed. No way to change your mind?"

"No Graham, this is my last trip. I didn't bring phones. And back home I'll be looking for new fields to till. Don't know what. Maybe something to do with white collar crimes, especially individuals in companies that exploit workers. Haven't worked it out yet."

Our meal arrives, and we eat in silence. I'm pleasantly surprised by my entrée. Maybe giving Graham the bad news has lifted a cloud, or maybe it's just the right chef on the right night. We empty the wine, and I suggest limoncello to finish off. Gina is busy so I pick up the drinks from the bar.

At last, both satiated, we stand and shake hands. Graham says, "I'll miss hearing about your work, Derwent. It's been a great partnership. I just wish it could have lasted longer."

There's nothing for me to say beyond "Thanks for the meal,

Graham, I wish you well." I bow my head slightly to convey my respect.

With that he turns and leaves. We always leave at separate times and take different paths back to our boats. I have no idea whether he's moored in the same marina as me or in one of several others that are available in this town. I suspect since he's originally from the area, that he knows local mooring spots that aren't publicly advertised.

I nurse a black coffee unhurriedly and leave ten minutes later when Gina is in the kitchen. I'm always intent on minimizing others' recollections of my visit.

The evening is mild, the first stars appearing as the moon sits sentinel just above the horizon.

I 'm relieved our meeting is over.

I pause and absorb the evening's treasures above.

The shrill siren of an emergency vehicle not far away shatters my reverie. It quickly comes closer. Three blocks from my marina a crowd is gathered on a street corner. The blaring ambulance stops there and EMTs spill out of the rear doors. I get a glimpse of a man lying on the ground as the first responders bend down to assist.

I stop, kitty corner at the intersection, and watch. If ever in the same situation, I want these medics. They administer oxygen and apply CPR furiously. Scissors to the shirt exposes the man's chest. Goop. Clear. A couple hundred joules rocks his heart, but the outcome is preordained. Two shocks later one of the medics shakes his head and puts his coat over the man's face and chest.

I could have told tell them their efforts would be in vain, but I walk on. Hopefully they'll put the chap's death down to an unexpected heart attack.

Which it was.

Even in its diluted form, my poison cocktail always works perfectly, albeit slower in a strong liqueur.

Rules of Hunting

Chapter 1

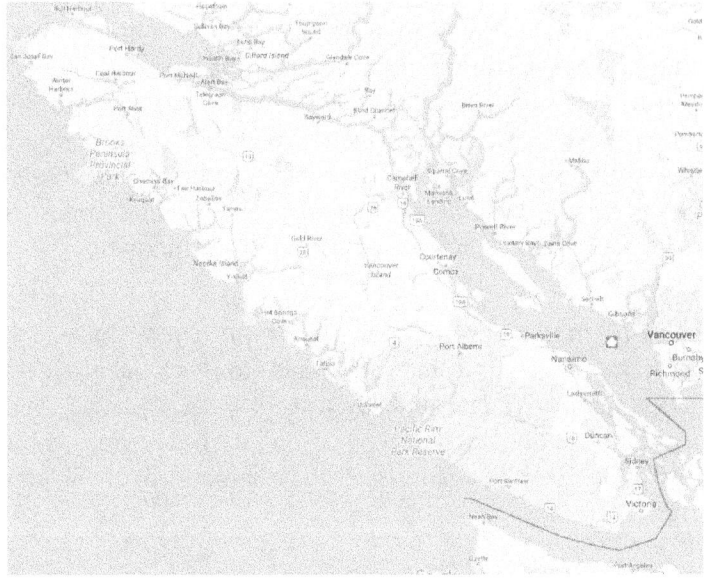

God must have been angry the day he created Vancouver Island.

If one looks at a map that shows the whole island, one sees that in forming it, He used a giant carving knife to create the four awesome passages of water which now skirt and define the land mass. Johnstone Strait, the Strait of Georgia, Haro Strait, and the Strait of Juan de Fuca are deep incisions that have cleanly removed connections the new island might have once had with British Columbia and the State of Washington.

Even after its creation God must have remained unhappy, for it looks like He hacked away with his formation knife at the southwest and northwest coast of the island, creating all sorts of inlets from Port Renfrew in the south to San Josef Bay in the north. And to add insult to injury He wielded two final slashes that came close to severing the northern and southern tips of the island. Extending the northern Rupert Inlet from its head at Washlawlis Creek 5 more miles to the Keogh Shoals, just south of the Port Hardy airport, would have created a tricky byway and another small blunt-shaped northwest island for the originating First Nation tribes. It looks like God must have relented at the last moment.

Similarly, in the south He cleaved a mighty 40 mile long northerly passage from Port Beale to Port Alberni. He stopped short of Dunsmuir by just 14 miles. Maybe He'd finally gotten tired, and instead of long slashes He settled for poking holes in the landscape that became lakes in later days.

Whatever the original reasons were for creating the island, the First Nations people found it a wonderful place to live. The open seas gave them salmon, shellfish, and whales, the pristine forests sheltered furred animals, from rabbits to deer to bears. Food and clothing were plentiful. And a relatively mild climate with annual snowfalls ranging from 13 inches in the south to 28 inches in the north, along with summer temperatures rarely exceeding 80 degrees Fahrenheit across the island were very tolerable.

The white man similarly found the island attractive. For both residing and retiring, as well as for boating and hunting. It was the latter sport that had my partner, John, and I making our second pilgrimage to Port Alberni from where we planned to undertake a five-day black bear hunting trip. We'd motored up from Seattle in my 50ft express cruiser, clearing customs in Victoria, then dealing with nasty winds in the Strait of Juan de Fuca. The constant heavy westerly gusts had made for a slow, rough, high-seas ride, and we were thankful when we finally turned northeast into Barkley Sound and found protection behind Diana and Shelby Islands before pulling into Bamfield for a rest and afternoon snack.

Forty miles from the ocean at the head of the inlet we cut our throttles to no-wake speed and waited nearly twenty minutes to get a VHF response from the dockmaster at the Port Alberni China Creek Marina. Jared met us at the outside slip to which we'd been assigned, but after fastening one line to a dock cleat, he went running back to the office. We could see flashing police car lights in the parking lot and wondered what was going on.

The cops certainly weren't there to welcome us.

Chapter 2

John and I worked for an independent security firm in Seattle. Our company was hired variously by corporations, transport groups, city administrative councils, sports venues, and even police departments when they needed extra officers on duty around contentious local events. As security enforcers we didn't have police powers but had the ability to restrain and detain folks who were violating the law in some way or creating a public nuisance.

John and I had been involved in a recent incident which had cast a semi-black mark over our services, and we were glad to be gone from the home scene where various forms of support and liberal hysteria were being played out. We were temporarily on leave, not suspended per se, but encouraged to be absent for a bit. Suited us perfectly.

John and I are both big, 2 and 3 inches over 6ft, with similar builds, having both been linebackers in our college football teams, each weighing in around 225 lbs. We had lots in common, one relevant aspect being that we each had two daughters, mine aged 10 and 12, John's 11 and 14. For both of us, the girls were a major source of pride and joy. All four were smart, athletic, nice looking, pleasant kids.

With one big difference. John and his girls were black, whereas I, and my two, were white.

Our colour difference worked well in altercations we dealt with. To stop some of the potential cries and accusations of racial nonsense, John approached black violators, while I approached white ones.

We were heading back to headquarters on one of the Lake Union trams when a black punk boarded, unsteady on his feet, his body twitching, a jambox cradled in one arm blasting rap. John and I both tensed, anticipating trouble. An older gentleman asked the kid to turn his music off, but the punk simply turned and spat on him, and raised his fist in a striking motion. A brazen white teenage girl bravely stepped between the gent and the punk's heavy punch which caught her full on her right breast, and she crumpled over, howling in distress. John was ahead of me striding from the back of the tram where we'd been standing. He wrapped his arms around the punk and wrested the jambox away. It fell to the floor and the gent in question turned it off. I bent down to the girl and held her shoulders as she cradled her arms across her chest, tears streaming down her cheeks. The tram stopped, I called 911, and we half escorted, half carried, the punk and his victim to the sidewalk, while the tram continued on.

I wrapped my jacket over the girl's shoulders and managed to get her name, Carrie, and home phone number, as we waited for the ambulance to show. She seemed to be regaining her composure, so I turned my attention to John and the assailant, who was struggling in his arms and swearing loudly. The creep managed to turn and spit at John, just as he had on the tram. That disgusting action immediately raised the wrath level in both of us.

The fact that he had hurt the innocent girl invoked specters of our own daughters being accosted, and that was too much. While John held the punk I kneed him heavily in the groin and his struggles ceased as he bent over.

It was John's turn. I held the druggie and John smashed the heels of his fists against the kid's temples, pounding the crystals in his middle ears to alternate internal destinations. It would be a long while before he heard rap again.

My turn. The kid tried to raise his hands to his ears, leaving his torso unprotected. My right fist jarred deep against his right kidney.

John's turn again. A frightening cracking noise indicated a finger on the kid's left hand had been broken. He crumpled at John's feet moaning incoherently and we pulled him into a sitting position in a doorway, just as a police car and ambulance announced their arrival.

No question, our treatment of the punk constituted 'excessive force'. A citizen on the tram had caught some of our initial actions there on a cell phone video camera. That stood us in good stead later against a couple of bystanders' versions of what had taken place on the sidewalk. The young girl was a heroine. Her mother met her at the hospital, from which she was released after examination and a couple of painkillers. The punk was left to his own devices once we told the cops our version of the incident. We have no idea what happened to his jambox.

Thank heavens we didn't make true headline news. More like page three news, but of course, being Seattle, one-eyed liberal left-wingers came out of the woodwork looking for any possible and implausible reason to persecute us. Black force on a black assailant gave their positions limited political credibility, and a brave white girl standing up to a black drug-addicted creep mitigated the pathetic trouble makers' rhetoric and arguments. Online and TV coverage died out in two days.

John and I had no regrets, and welcomed the support we got inside our company. The police smartly avoided any public comment. We understood how our bosses had to show concern publicly over our actions, while knowing full well that any internal investigation would be short, and contain only a mild rebuke.

Chapter 3

At the China Creek Marina dock we added bow and stern lines to dock cleats, and switched off the engines. The multitude of blue and red lights in the marina parking lot raised our curiosity from both a personal and professional point of view. Based on stories we'd heard from the Washington State water police, we regarded the Royal Canadian Mounted Police, or RCMP, as a highly competent organization.

Unfortunately, the assistant at the marina office who handled our registration didn't know anything beyond the fact that the police had arrived just forty minutes earlier and were investigating a specific car in the lot.

In response to our questions she said, "The dockmaster you met handed over the marina's current record book and the police thumbed through it looking to see if the car was listed in the previous two weeks."

"Do you know why they were interested in finding it?" I asked.

"They didn't say, although they found no indication of it being registered here. They took the book away. I'll need to record your information on a slip of paper for now and enter it later when we get the record book back."

"No problem," I countered. "What do you need to know?"

We provided our names, cell phone numbers, boat details and customs clearance permit number, paid cash for 4 days moorage fees, and prepared to leave.

The girl wanted to talk, for she spoke up as we turned to go. "Of course, anyone can drive in and park. Giving us details before leaving on a boat isn't required, and parking is free. Who knows who parks out there for what reason?"

Something in her tone and words hinted at nervousness. Our departmental sensitivity training kicked in and registered a need to listen.

"There seems to be a surprising number of police cars out there," I ventured. "Must be something serious."

She looked at me directly, then hesitated for a few seconds. Finally, she blurted out, "I'm wondering if it's the getaway car used by the two men who raped and beat those three college girls in the last few days."

Chapter 4

We'd always thought Port Alberni was a pleasant, off-the-track, quiet little town. Maybe a few domestic disputes each year, bouts of offensive drunkenness, the inevitable car accidents, some illegal hunting episodes, breaking and entering, but nothing of a heavy crime nature. Sure, unemployment was variable because the seasonal lumber and fishing industries dominated the job scene.

Kayaking, sport fishing, hunting, and mountain bike riding were activities that attracted tourists, and local residents even had a branch of North Island College to pursue select academic courses. There were numerous creeks and ravines that cut through the city to create natural barriers; the hiking trails in the associated parks added tremendously to the quality of life in the town.

Rapes were a rarity in Port Alberni. The girl behind the office counter was very upset. Before we could respond to her outburst she added, "One of the students stayed with our family last year. She was very sweet."

John was super empathic. "That's so awful. The poor girls must be absolutely devastated. I feel so bad for them. What a horrible crime. I have two daughters, the eldest just a couple of years younger than you. I can imagine how this must have affected you."

A look of understanding flashed across the girl's face. "I just hope the brutes are found quickly and dealt with. They held fish knives to the girls' throats, and one of them almost killed the boyfriend of one girl after forcing him to watch. The boy and two girls are still in the hospital."

I nodded sympathetically as I thought about my two daughters, friends of John's girls. In fact it was because of our daughters' friendships that John and I had come together. Before, we were in competitive security companies.

I spoke up. "Like my friend here, I have daughters and I worry about them all the time. From the moment they were born I was conscious of the risks of SIDS, crossing the road alone, being bullied at school, and being abused physically. Do you have someone you trust whom you can talk to?"

She mouthed 'yes'.

I was conscious of not pushing the lass too far, but the protective side of me wanted to know more about the perpetrators.

"Were the victims able to describe their assailants?"

"Oh yes, you can see their images on the Wanted Posters on the noticeboard behind you. I guess they were made up from police identikits. I hate looking at them, the ugly creeps!"

John and I spent several minutes examining the pictures. We had to agree with the assessment. Both men looked to be in their late thirties or early forties, with dark unkempt hair, one top more curly than the other, and straggly beards. The slightly younger-looking chap had a short vertical scar on his left cheek, the other one's nose appeared to have been broken, as it wasn't straight. But their eyes were similar in shape, and it wouldn't be hard to conclude they were brothers. There was a hint of indigenous ancestry in their face shapes and dimensions, but they were predominantly Caucasian.

 "I sure hope they are gone for everyone's sake," I said.

John added, "I'm sure the Mountie organization will find them. I doubt they are locals. May even have arrived by boat and stolen the car that's being examined."

Turning to me, he said, "Pete, I think it's time we left."

And turning to the girl he added, "Good luck to you miss. Hang in there. We'll be back."

Chapter 5

Port Alberni is surrounded by mountains covered in Douglas fir, hemlock, yellow cedar and western red cedar. The forests and meadows are home to large Roosevelt Elk, Black Bears, Mountain Lions, and Blacktail Deer, so the area is a veritable hunter's paradise. John and I had arrived in the last week of April, hoping to bag a black bear each.

On our previous visit we had hired a guide associated with a local outfitter, but decided that this time we would try hunting on our own. We knew we didn't have the experience a guide had, but this was our time away, banished from work, to do as we wished, and we looked forward to hunting unaided.

Back at the boat, we checked the regional maps and our BC Hunting authorizations for Limited Entry Hunting, and packaged them together in a clear plastic bag. We reviewed each other's clothing, making sure we were ready for cold temperatures in the mountains, then organized our food supplies and all the camping accessories. We made sure our guns, a 30-06 and .35 Winchester, were secure, and that our 220 grain ammunition was dry and safe.

Next was something new. Electric Fat bikes. We were excited to try out their relatively new technology. Bikes with electric motors and wide 4" tires at low pressure that were designed in part for riding over narrow dirt trails.

John had first suggested them. "Look Pete, where we're going has a myriad of logging trails, and decommissioned and recontoured roads. Most will be unused and overgrown in places admittedly, but still providing relatively easy access to areas. Being motorized, these bikes will save us a lot of energy we'd otherwise use peddling regular mountain bikes up steep climbs."

We visited several bike outlets in the greater Seattle area, liking what we saw more and more. I told John, "I like the fact that we can ride these bikes across muddy ground, even snow. It's possible we could get snow in the areas around Port Alberni in April. The bikes are geared for rough terrain which we'll strike for sure. And the wide tires give good traction. Damned smart machines."

John liked other attributes. "With low pressure in the tires they'll let us ride right over small branches and rocks. Those would be obstacles for normal mountain bikes. Plus, being electric, they are surprisingly quiet. I think even bears would have to be pretty close to hear them. These are just the ticket."

We found a brand that also offered a single wheel cargo carrier that could attach to the back wheel and frame, so we bought one for each bike. Outbound, we planned to use only one of the carriers for our tent and provisions. Inbound we hoped we'd be pulling bear meat and skins on the second carrier. At least, those were our dreams.

Chapter 6

We were downing our second cups of after-dinner coffee when we were hailed from the pier. It was the dockmaster, who had briefly tied our midship line when we arrived. "Hi gents. Just about to go off duty, but wanted to apologize for my quick disappearance earlier today. Had quite a scene here as you probably saw." He extended his hand and introduced himself. "I'm glad you're staying with us. Going hunting by the looks of your gear."

We shook hands and offered him coffee, which he accepted. Young chap, maybe 30 years old, facial skin clear, blonde wavy hair, friendly blue eyes. Easy conversationalist. "I gather Stephanie in the office filled you in a little. The cops think that car might have been used by the two rapist thugs. No concrete proof yet. Turns out the car was stolen from another marina up the road four days ago but wasn't reported missing until the owner got back from his fishing trip this morning."

John worked to get a word in. "Those guys sound like truly nasty fellows. Stephanie was pretty shook up about their acts."

"And she doesn't know everything, or she'd be in even worse shape. My brother was one of the cops who came by today. He told me that after beating and raping two of the girls, they cut their breasts and pudenda pretty badly. Those girls will likely have scars for life. Plus they took the girls' underwear as souvenirs. That's not public of course. For some reason the third girl was not cut as badly. Her boyfriend took the punishment instead."

The description made me want to puke.

"What sick bastards!" I exclaimed. "Just as well they're not here this minute. They might be leaving with a few deep cuts themselves. Absolute cunts!"

John remained a bit more rational, although I knew he was most likely seething underneath as well. "So presumably the Canadian Coast Guard is out looking for them? We didn't notice any official boats on our way up here."

"Well, the marinas are all trying to identify which boat must have been theirs. That would help both the RCMP and the Coast Guard. Problem is, it's the start of tourist season and lots of boats arrived in the last week. Even at the best of times not all get registered correctly, and many of our resident owners, who would have noted the arrival of a new visiting vessel, are working at their jobs during the day, and are not down at the marina. My brother says the men in the force are aghast at the crime and can't wait to catch the guys. Nothing like this has happened in decades around here."

With that, Jared rose to leave. "Gotta go, the missus will be wondering where I am. Are you off early in the morning?"

I responded with a smile. "Yep, can't keep those bears waiting too long."

"Well, I'll also be out hunting them mid May, which is when I get a week off. This early in the season I'd stay low in the river valleys rather than high on the mountains. And black bears only, no grizzlies per island law, although I hear a couple have been sighted in the region. Unusual for them to be found this far south on the island.   Good luck chaps. See you when you get back.   We'll look after your boat meanwhile."

And with that he leapt back up on the dock and was gone.

Chapter 7

The sun was sending its first light onto the tops of the snow-covered peaks as we finished our bacon and eggs. Large pads of butter on thick country toast disappeared easily, and we quaffed down our coffee, anxious and excited to get going. It took a little muscle to maneuver the 60 lb bikes from boat to dock but we quickly worked out a system and in thirty minutes had our tent, rifles, food, water, and other gear firmly stowed on the cargo trailer attached to my machine. We took a couple of spins around the parking lot to see how the trailer performed, but after stopping once and tightening some of the ropes holding the load, we were ready to go.

There were only 4 vehicles parked at the trail head we'd selected, 3 pickup trucks and a small RV. Still early in the season of course, and in a way we were pleased. John voiced thoughts that matched mine. "Looks like minimal competition for bears, Pete. Especially since there are several trails to choose from. The southeasterly one we want starts over there near that big stone pile and marker." We'd picked this particular trail since it seemed to lead to multiple options for valley and river touring as opposed to a lot of high peak travelling, although one couldn't avoid hill climbing entirely. As well, the targeted area allowed access to several different Government Hunting Management Units and included easy-to-avoid First Nation territories.   We were trying to make our trip without a guide as easy on ourselves as possible.

I led the way so John could keep an eye on the trailer. The bikes performed flawlessly, with our first stop after nearly an hour occurring where the old logging trail we were on crossed a small brook.   We were at the edge of a forest, but could see open meadows and clear cuts in the distance.

"These pines smell so good," I remarked. "This brings back memories from our last visit."

John nodded his head in agreement. "And we're moving much faster on these bikes than we did on the horses last time. We must have covered at least 6 or 7 miles already."

The meadows stretched across small rolling hills for a couple of miles with the track undulating mildly, providing an easy ride. By lunch time we'd put 15 miles behind us, so we stopped for a well-earned break by another stream that was meandering downhill to a creek we could see in a small ravine.

A salad, followed by ham and cheese rolls, an apple, and cool water refreshed us as we relaxed and enjoyed the warm sunshine, each wrapped in our own reverie. Suddenly John whispered, "Pete – check out the creek!"   I looked up and there 500 yards away, uphill from us, two black bears were having a drink. I quickly reached back for my rifle, but John was ahead of me. He checked the rangefinder – 478 yards – and decided there'd be closer opportunities elsewhere. "That's an awfully long shot for a novice like me," he said, and reluctantly closed down his bipod stand.

Still, it was exciting to see potential targets, even if so far away. We were clearly in bear country. A rewarding sign in itself. We watched the bears for 5 minutes as they ambled along the creek, eventually disappearing into the woods beyond. A thrilling start to our adventure.

About 4 pm we started to feel a little sore in the saddle, so began to look for a campsite. We picked a spot at the edge of a grove of fir trees and set up our tent. I rounded up some dry twigs and branches for firewood while John went off in search of a stream with running water. I had a nice blaze going by the time John returned, but from the scrunched-up look on his face I could tell something was bothering him.

"So much for a lack of competition Pete. Around the corner of that hillock up ahead I spotted smoke drifting up through the trees. We've got company less than a mile away. Amazing! I feel like our space has been invaded, even though the hunters or hikers in the camp were obviously here ahead of us."

I must say I wasn't particularly happy at the news. Irritated that our planned isolation and solitude was no longer the case, but also a tad concerned on other grounds. Despite the fact that we wore orange vests for safety, I always worried when there were other hunters in the vicinity.

"Best thing John, is that we have early dinner, then go over and meet whoever's camped there. Maybe they'll have some tips for us on finding bear in these parts. And we alert them to our presence so we avoid getting shot at. I'm sure we'll be well gone next day."

"Could be Roosevelt Elk hunters as well, Pete. Boy I'd love to see one of those big ones up close."

Long shadows fell over us but the sun was still providing plenty of light as it shone above the tree line on nearby hills. We slung our guns across our backs and walked in the direction of the nearby camp.   About 100 yards away from where the smoke was drifting lazily upward, we started shouting.

"Ahoy there."

"Hello."

"Hi there."

"Coming along the trail."

"Anyone there?"

We kept this up until with 25 yards of the fire but we got no response whatsoever. We assumed the campers wouldn't have left a fire actively burning if they'd gone off somewhere, so the scene was puzzling. I turned nervously to John.

"I don't like this buddy. I wonder what on earth is going on."

Chapter 8

30 more paces and the situation became abundantly clear. On either side of the fire, two untidy males sprawled in the dirt, one on his back, the other on his side. Both were unconscious from drink, as empty bottles of Canadian Club and Black Velvet whiskies were close by their bodies. Two tin dishes showed the remains of a meat dinner. The chap laying on his back had soiled his pants where he'd peed himself. His partner had upchucked a small quantity of liquid and food. The place smelled of stale liquor, vomit, charcoal, and smoke.

Both men sported beards that looked about 3 days old, one's baseball cap still held firm, the other's was almost off, its rear buckle buried in leafy debris. Aside from the orange hats, they both wore camouflage outfits and heavy mountaineering boots. Their rifles leaned against the front wheels of a two-man ATV which was covered in dust and a few straggly cedar branches. In a small trailer hitched behind the ATV was a pile of meat, partially covered with a tarp, and tied down with ropes. A few flies buzzed around the cart.

John and I conversed in normal tones, but neither man woke up. One snored and snorted every now and then, although his mate remained quiet. It certainly wasn't what we had expected. Gross, was my immediate reaction. I spotted what looked like a well-trodden pathway leading downhill from the ATV, and decided to check it out. I hadn't gone 20 yards when I spotted one end of a thick rope line tied around a nine-inch diameter tree trunk. The line stretched into thick brush and was well-concealed from any casual observer. As I traced along the rope I came across the skin of a black bear. This was a large bear – trophy-sized. A fine catch indeed.

But what I found next dismayed me. Here was a huge brown skin, nearly double the size of the brown fur. These guys had clearly bagged one of the grizzlies Jared had mentioned. Huge, and totally illegal. I felt disgusted at the wanton killing of such a fine protected beast. I hastened back to the clearing and fetched John to witness the carnage.

"These guys are rogues Pete. I don't think we want anything to do with them. Hunters who think they are above the law. Guess they'll leave the grizzly's meat behind when they pull back to a trailhead somewhere, so it can't be identified. What a pair of creeps. Do we report them?"

"Don't know John. But maybe we could check to see if they have any ID in case we do end up turning them in. What a pair of shits. This whole scene makes me sick. Let's check their tent, then I vote for back tracking a couple of miles, even though we are tired. I don't want to be near these louts."

I thought of taking a photo, although with the bushes crowding the line and the failing light, it wouldn't come out well. I replaced my phone in the large zip pocket on the front of my pants.

John and I pulled the tent flaps aside, peered inside and nearly threw up as we withdrew. Two mattresses side by side on the ground, but it what was overhead that took our breath away. Hanging from the roof mid-line were three bras and three panties. Incredible!

We'd caught up with the rapists of Port Alberni!

We were both shocked, looking at each other wide-eyed and speechless.

Suddenly, I was no longer a hunter, but a father of two girls. What if one of my girls had been raped? I'd want to kill the bastard responsible. The two turds who cut up the girls in Port Alberni were here, not twenty feet away, drunk unconscious out of their minds.

John and I had shared enough about our families as we worked together for me to know he was likely having similar thoughts to mine. Neither of us tried to conceal our disgust. This was abominable! The rapists hadn't left town by boat, but were in the back country hunting! Vile specimens of humanity.

I pulled my phone out and this time took several photos. What a gross sense of celebration this pair had. Showing off their trophies where they slept. I felt myself becoming angrier and angrier. Murder was in my heart.

John pulled me back outside the tent, and I stored the camera again. "What do we do?" I whispered. His strong hand gripped my arm and led me away out of normal voice range of the two creeps, just in case they might wake and hear us, although they still hadn't moved.

"We need to tie them up Pete so they can't get away, take their weapons, and then go inform the police. Too bad our phones don't work here." I nodded my understanding, then thought of something. "We can use the ropes around the meat on the ATV cart. You go start loosening them while I search for their ammunition."

Regretfully, I went back to the tent, checked under the mattresses and found my target – two boxes of ammunition, one unopened, the other half empty. Seeing the girls' underwear again brought bile to my throat. I left as quickly as possible and joined John at the ATV, where I removed the key from the ignition and pocketed it. There were two bloody fish knives on the seat which they'd clearly used for skinning. I wanted to throw them away knowing they'd been used on humans as well, but for the moment I left them untouched. I did wonder, 'why fish knives?,' not hunting knives. All I could reason was that they wanted to mislead victims into thinking they were fishermen when they weren't. I didn't dwell further on it.

The small toolbox on the ATV contained a couple of wrenches and screwdrivers, as well as a big roll of duct tape. I raised the latter in front of John's eyes, pulled out three inches of tape and brushed it across my lips while pointing to the men by the fire. The idea was obvious to him. I whipped out my Havalon Evolve multi-tool and cut two ten inch lengths of the sticky silver tape.

It was time to make the lives of these drunken creeps far more uncomfortable.

Chapter 9

Darkness was falling now and it was getting harder to see detail. The embers were dying and the ring of light they threw was becoming smaller and smaller. We decided to tackle the guy on his side first.

We advanced quietly up to our victim who still seemed fast asleep. At a quick signal John grabbed the chap's head, turned it up and I plastered the duct tape across his mouth and face. He blinked once, but that was it. I couldn't believe how drunk he must have been. I tied one length of rope around his ankles, weaving it in and out between his legs, and knotting it behind him, while John did the same with the chap's arms. It took more effort with them as one of his arms had to be pulled back underneath him. I helped John tip the fiend on his stomach. We then tied his arms at the elbows as well as at the wrists.

He was starting to wake out of his stupor and began twisting his body back and forth, muttering behind his mouth tape. I'd stayed under control as we prepared to capture the pair, but could no longer hold myself in check. Without hesitation I kicked the bastard hard in the side of his face and heard bone crunch. He twisted sideways to avoid a second blow and I noticed the scar on his face that was evident in the Wanted Posters. His move provided the perfect opportunity for another hard kick, this time to his abdomen. He grunted in pain, and for the moment stopped squirming.

The noise had registered with his companion who was now struggling to wake himself up. He lifted himself on his elbows and looked at us in a quizzical way. "Who're you?" he rasped. John moved quickly to the chap's side and punched him in the face with a heavy blow. We had both served in the reservists at some stage and had participated in exercises and training that made us both highly competent in hand to hand combat. John's fist knocked the guy out and we proceeded to gag him and tie him up like his partner.

John turned to me. "We need to make sure neither one can undo the knots on the other's bonds, so we should tie them

to different trees before we leave."

I didn't disagree but my mind was elsewhere. Trussing up the two shits had gotten the adrenaline going for sure, but similarly to earlier, it had also prompted other thoughts and feelings. In a way I felt dirty just touching the creeps. They'd raped three innocent college girls and then tortured them further by carving cuts in sensitive female places that would stay reminders for life. One thing was the exercise of brute male dominance and indecency, another was the gross act of inflicting pain and utter brutality just for the sake of it. What if two of the girls had been my daughters? Life would have changed dramatically for both me and the girls.

My blood started to boil as I thought more. My anger rose to a height I'd never experienced before.

"There's one more thing we have to do John," I blurted.

"And that's make sure these shits never rape anyone again."

John knew immediately what I was thinking. If we stopped and thought deeply about the consequences we'd probably never proceed. Mentally we'd already foregone that option, so without any hesitation we both hurried back to the ATV and retrieved the two fish knives and the duct tape.

Part of me wanted to shoot the two shits, but I rationalized that that would be too good for them. Preferably, I wanted them to suffer for the rest of their lives.

I also wanted them to feel the terror their victims must have experienced when assaulted. Both were wide awake now, struggling with their bonds, their yells stifled by the gags we'd put in place. I sat on the slightly bigger guy's chest and waved a blood-stained knife in front of his eyes. Using slowly paced, deliberately chosen words, I said, "You raped those innocent girls you scum, and I'm going to make sure you can never do that again. I'm going to cut your dick off and leave it for the crows. Do you want a quick job, or should I take my time?"

The pleading look in his eyes, and the frantic yells, were the reward I needed. I moved backwards and sat on his legs, then reached forward, undid his belt and pulled his soiled pants and drawers down to his knees. The yells got louder as I wiped the knife across his bare belly. Fear, coupled with disbelief, showed in his eyes. Perfect.

I wedged his legs apart with my boot and with one quick slice relieved him of the last inch and a half of his dick, held it up to his face as he howled and cried, and then threw it into the last coals of the fire. John handed me two strips of duct tape which I wrapped tightly around his stub, stopping the bleeding.

My feelings were numb. Justice had been served.

After a few words of condemnation, John followed suit with the second monster. This one blacked out for a few seconds with his loss.

All over, there were no high-fives between us, just grim looks of acceptance and job complete.

We dragged one fellow, then the other, to sitting positions by two stout trees. The protests were subdued as they surveyed their maimed bodies. Their bare butts were on the ground, unprotected by clothes, so they could readily witness their new state. We trussed them securely so they were hardly able to move.

John and I sat on our haunches, emotionally drained, pondering our exit.

Chapter 10

A rising three-quarter moon offered a weak light as we looked at each other in silence, gradually getting our breaths back. We had to leave, but first I rose and placed the rogues' identical guns across their legs and showed them the ammunition I'd taken.   There was murder in their eyes.

"We have the GPS coordinates for this location, so we'll send the police for you in the morning guys. I have the key to your vehicle so I'd be patient as you wait for help. Try and have a good night."

With that we left. Once out of range of our victims' hearing John spoke up. "Guess we just ruined out best-laid plans for hunting bear Pete. We have no option but to break camp and head back to the marina. I'm just glad we bought those high intensity LED lamps for our bikes. Even so it will be near dawn before we get there. Going to make it a long day and night buddy."

I murmured my assent, said nothing else for the moment. I'm sure John was as conscious as I was of just how extreme our actions were. Excessive force? Oh yes. No question about it. But at least no more daughters anywhere would be violated by these two. For the moment however neither of us wanted to think about the potential consequences of being held accountable for our misdeeds.

We broke down our camp, piled the tent on the cargo trailer and set off on the long trip back to civilization. As each of us became fatigued we let the other go first, changing leadership positions like geese do when they fly in a group. Because of the semi darkness we were unable to see every rock and depression in the trail, so had a few minor mishaps, but after hours of riding we finally pulled into the parking lot at the trailhead.

It was eerily quiet, with two extra vehicles present that weren't there before. Even here there was no cell signal for our phones, although there was a public phone on a wall inside a large shelter. After using the attached facilities and washing our hands and faces in ice-cold water, we sat and rested on one of the benches at a large wooden picnic table.

"Dammit John. Who knows what will happen if we're caught, but I'd still do it again. What a despicable pair those two were. I hope they regret their actions every day for the rest of their lives."

"Yep, me too Pete. But let's not sit around here. We need to get back to the boat ASAP. Before we leave though I'm going to use that phone and call 911 with the GPS coordinates of the bastards' camp. I'll mask my voice as best as I can but I'm not sure what I can say that will cause them to respond immediately to go check out some vague spot in the wilderness. Pity in a way that we can't use your cellphone to send those pictures of undergarments. That would convince them."

"Why not wait till we get back to the boat to call?" I asked.

"Because if they trace the call to this phone they'll think we left here by car or truck or RV. Might help us a little."

"Well, your brain is certainly working better than mine, buddy, I'll admit. I'd tell them we came across two hunters who seem to have shot a grizzly, and who look like the images we'd seen on a Wanted Poster for the rapists. It'll be up to them to decide whether to follow-through or not. I think having two reasons will be sufficient to send at least one mounted chap out to investigate."

"Ok, I'll be back in a minute, then we need to hustle back to the boat before all those coffee-drinking captains are up and about. Speaking of which, a hot brew would certainly go down well. Guess we'll just have to wait a little longer."

Chapter 11

No-one seemed to be awake on the pier where we were moored. Even so, we worked hard to minimize any noise as we undid our cargo carrier and put the bikes back on the boat. We didn't tidy everything back in place to the same degree of organization as our outbound-journey arrangements.

We sat quietly on the rear deck watching the first ducks fly over, sipping hot coffee that tasted absolutely wonderful. That is, until John put his cup down abruptly and raised a pair of binoculars to his eyes. His head pivoted slowly as he tracked something in his line of sight directed toward the marina office. His face was intense as he watched for about four or five minutes saying nothing. Suddenly he grinned, muttered "yes" triumphantly, put down the glasses and rushed off the boat. I watched him run along the connecting piers, bent half-over, wondering what on earth he was up to.

To my surprise he ran up the steps to the door of the marina office, and opened it with a quick turn of the knob. He was inside for one or two minutes, then the door opened and he eased down the steps, and headed back my way.

He was smiling as he climbed back on board. Panting, he reached in his coat pocket and handed me a crumpled piece of paper. "Something to definitely treasure, my friend."

He was right. It was the piece of paper the office assistant had filled out when we arrived. On it were our names, boat name, phone numbers, boat details, customs clearance permit number, and how much we were being charged for moorage.

"You are something else!" I exclaimed. "Great thinking. What triggered that run to the office and back?"

"Well, I saw a small car enter the parking lot, which was no big thing on its own, but the fact that it drove all the way to the back kept my attention. A woman got out, so I used the binocs to see where she was headed. As I got a better focus on her I realized it was Stephanie and that she was arriving to open up the office.

"The lights went on inside, and I could see her shadow on the shades as she moved around to a couple of spots. Whatever she was doing suddenly got stopped in its tracks, for she came out the door putting her coat on, and headed back towards her car. Presumably she forgot to bring something with her to the office."

I got it. "So you saw the door was unlocked and wondered if you'd have enough time to try and locate our arrival data and remove it. Brilliant thinking my friend. You go to the top of your class."

"Thanks Pete. It means there's no 'official' record of our visit here. Jared and Stephanie will both have memories of us if ever questioned, but there is nothing written to share with the police. Jared will know the type of boat, but probably not its name. Time for us to move on."

The current was ebbing, so we pushed off the outer dock where we were moored and silently drifted out into the main body of water until we were well free of the marina before starting our engines. It's certainly possible that we'd been seen leaving, but not because we'd made any noise doing so. We had forty miles ahead of us to think about our next moves before we reached the Pacific Ocean. Plenty of time to work something out.

Chapter 12

We were tired from lack of sleep but didn't dare to nap one at a time. We needed all four eyes actively watching for floating logs on the way southwest. About twenty minutes out a speedboat came tearing by in the opposite direction. His wake rocked us a little, and as I watched him disappear in the distance I wondered what marina he was headed to.   I unfolded the paper map we had as backup to our electronic navigation system and identified the four distinct marinas back in town. The one we'd stayed at was 7 miles south of one right by the town center, and there were two more two miles further to the north, actually in the Somass river. A new idea was forming in my mind and I asked John to cut the engines so I could share it more easily with him.

"What if we turned back and headed for the Clutesi Haven Marina 9 miles north of where we stopped the last two nights? That's a totally different part of town, where it's unlikely anyone from the China Creek Marina would see us. We'd still have two days for hunting, we'd just head for a different region than before and hope to get luckier sooner rather than later."

"Hmm, not a bad idea Pete, but what if the dockmaster asks how come we are arriving so early?"

"Well, we could say we stayed at Bamfield and left there real early in order to get deep on the hunting trails by mid-afternoon. A bit misleading, but I could live with it."

"Me too. Plus we'd be way out in a totally different part of the countryside when any discovery is made of the two scumbags. I like that notion especially. Hang on while I turn our boat around my friend. You got the coordinates of that marina handy? I'll put them into the system. Let's go."

A nice clean marina with water and 50 amp power greeted us as the sun rose to warm the day. No awkward questions were raised, just the natural curiosity ones of what we'd be hunting and how long we intended to stay. We paid for three days rather than two, anticipating we'd stay a bit longer if we needed extra time to hunt.

Still tired from our overnight excursion we napped for two hours and woke refreshed, anxious to be in bear country once again.

This time we planned to head west into Hunting Management Unit 1-7, the opposite direction to where we'd been previously in Unit 1-5.

Chapter 13

It didn't take long to get back into the swing of things. The fresh mountain air, the beautiful scenery, and the exercise, brought out our vitality once again. I found myself humming with pleasure as my trusty bike ascended each incline with ease and coasted downhill. We saw a herd of elk in the distance across a large ravine, and stopped and watched them for fifteen minutes through our binoculars as they grazed contentedly in a field by the edge of a large grove of pines.

About 4:30 pm as the sun was just starting to recede behind the western mountain tops we sighted our first black bears. A party of three, presumably mother, father and infant based on size differences. Just over 200 yards away downhill from the old logging road we were on. Certainly within shooting range, but neither of us had the heart to break up a family, so we watched for a few minutes, then moved on.

Not thirty minutes later, as the first evening shadows darkened and became well defined, a lone male wandered onto the road 125 yards ahead.   He stopped, turned his head and looked at us, holding us in his line of sight through a long stare.   John was on the lead bike, and stayed motionless while the big fella gave us the once over. Thank heavens we were downwind from him. When his nose and eyes were satisfied that we weren't a threat he turned his body 90 degrees and ambled along the road in the direction we were headed. It was as if he were leading us somewhere, although we didn't follow.

John unslung his rifle from across his back and quietly dismounted. He lined up the rifle, resting it on the handlebars, and loaded two bullets. The bear must have heard the clicking noises as the safety came off, but he didn't stray from his path.

I whispered to John, "Are you ready?" and he nodded his head up and down. I stepped to one side of the road and started yelling "Yahoo, Yahoo," as loudly as I could while waving my arms about wildly. I caught the bear's attention and he stopped. His head swiveled and looked back, at which point I walked to the other side of the road so he'd have to turn sideways to watch me. Which he did.

He paused, his flank exposed, and John's shot caught him well behind the shoulder blade. A perfect lung shot. The beast crumpled to the road, raising a small cloud of dust. He twitched once, then was still. "Great shot, John," I exclaimed, and rushed over, swatted his back and hugged him around the shoulders. "One shot. Superb. He isn't going to move. Let's go check him out."

We approached carefully, both guns loaded. Last thing we wanted was to be unprotected and find he was heavily injured, and ready to charge us. John poked him, and when there was no response, let out a throaty roar, "Got him!" and danced around the huge specimen. The celebration was well deserved and I let him be, shaking his hand just once as he circled the black furry body.

The light was fading fast but I managed a couple of grainy photos, declaring we'd take more in the morning. We set up our tent and camp just off the roadway, leaving John's giant trophy right where he fell. We'd skin him in the morning when the light was better.

Chapter 14

Next morning, after skinning John's trophy and piling the meat on our unused trailer, we left camp about 10 am and headed further inland. We agreed to give it two hours before selecting a different return route lower in the valleys. A decision that would prove to be very rewarding.

It was mid-afternoon when we spied three bears fishing in a small creek. They were having a wonderful time slashing at salmon leaping over rocks, occasionally catching one in mid-air. They were on the smaller side and we guessed they were females, so after watching for 15 minutes and taking some action videos we decided to move on. I was getting a bit anxious knowing we had only a few hours of daylight left. I wanted a bear rug as well as John.

We stopped for a drink at a large, widened turn-around spot in the road, and were amazed to hear horses snorting in the direction we were headed. Clearly multiple horses were coming our way. A guided hunting group perhaps?

No. Instead, two policemen suddenly came into view. They dismounted, tied their horses to a branch of a tree at the edge of the clearing and came over to chat with us.

"Afternoon men. Looks like a nice kill there. Only one? May we see your licenses please?" Friendly, but also officious.

One of the officers inspected the meat on our trailer closely, took off his gloves, and rubbed through the fur of the hide. "Nice and thick, good specimen. Where's home fellas?"

"Seattle," I responded. "Heading back tomorrow morning unless we don't get lucky for a second prize in the next few hours."

"Came by boat or pickup to carry those bikes?" the first chap asked.

"Boat," John replied. We're at the Clutesi Haven marina."

"Good spot. And we just might be able to help you find your next target. 500 yards back we spied a lone male, good size, uphill, beside a creek coming down and across the road. Easy to find. Maybe he'll still be there. Might want to sneak up quietly, you'll see the cut in the road easily from a distance."

Now no longer officious. Maybe they were fellow hunters when off duty. Definitely helpful.

"Thanks officers. We'll check it out."

They remounted, and with a cheery wave moved on. John and I both exhaled thankful sighs. No questions about where we'd been. No information imparted about criminals at large. No mention of a grizzly being shot. We shook hands and smiled.

And perhaps my chance for a bear was closer than I had thought.

As promised, the creek was easy to see a couple of hundred yards ahead. No bear in view but we parked our bikes, loaded the rifles, and walked slowly forward. Downhill, the creek meandered through a large open meadow, so we turned our attention uphill where the Mounties had indicated that they'd seen the bear. The meadow extended 75 yards up to a stand of fir trees, spaced sparsely initially, but growing more dense the higher the slope.

We crept forward, one on either side of the creek, until we reached the treeline, where we stopped. I was about to give up and turn back when John, clicked his fingers and pointed into the forest. I silently joined him, and once my eyes focused on the darkness of the forest I saw what John was pointing at. There was the bear stretching up, scratching his back against a thick fir tree. He must have been seven feet tall and only 50 yards away. I was amazed he hadn't heard us – probably too intent on getting rid of old fur and pests in his thick hair.

John set up the tripod as I hesitatingly switched off the safety and placed the barrel in the stirrup. I worked hard to control my breathing although I could smell my own sweat from the adrenaline rush. I forced myself to be patient as I waited for him to change his side-on position and drop to all fours facing away from the tree. He must have had a giant itch as I waited four or five minutes by John's count, until he'd finished his ablutions.

Once down he shook himself and looked directly at us. That was my cue as I figured any second he'd be moving on. I squeezed the trigger and saw a spurt of blood from his side, a little higher up than I had intended. He yelped a strange cry and started to move towards us. But it was a death throes stagger, not a revengeful attack romp, and after two or three paces he dropped to the ground.

"Congratulations Pete. Nice shot. You got him just in time. Let's go check him out."

John clapped me around the shoulders and pumped my hand up and down. I was shaking, my chest heaving up and down as I inhaled and exhaled large breaths trying to calm down. I felt great. I wouldn't be going home empty handed.

Chapter 15

It took ages to skin my kill and load the meat onto our trailer. There was so much we put two legs in a canvas bag and tied it across my back. And did the same for John. Heavy, but not heavy enough to slow us down. What did slow us down was managing the bumps and ruts and crevices and grass knells along the recontoured road as we carefully avoided tipping the trailers over.

Back at the trailhead we happily took a break. An RV rolled in and the man and woman came over to examine our hides and meat. They were very complimentary.

"You missed all the excitement in town," the man offered.

"What's that?" I asked.

"You knew about the rapists right?" the chap asked.

We nodded our heads up and down.

"Well, the Mounties found them way east of town in a forest. Big surprise. Everyone had assumed they'd left by boat but not so. That was what they wanted folks to believe. Apparently they were suffering from exposure as they were being treated at the local hospital. Same place their victims had gone to. I hope they all never met up. If I were one of those poor four I'd have been tempted one night to smother the bastards with a pillow, or worse. Glad I don't have daughters!"

I couldn't resist a shot. "Too bad someone didn't shoot the bastards. I might even have volunteered."

Our news provider continued. "Who knows?   Maybe the Mounties threatened them.   There   was   something unspecified in the report we heard on the radio. It said the two were treated for hypothermia and small injuries. The RMCP certainly were upbeat about capturing the pair. Oh yes, among all the charges they were organizing against them, apparently there'll be one totally unrelated to the crimes in town, because they shot a grizzly. A big NO NO as you are probably aware."

"Glad to hear they caught the creeps. I'm sure the local townspeople will heave giant sighs of relief. I just hope the girls can overcome things in time. My heart goes out to them."

"And the boy as well," John added. "What a nightmare for all of them."

"Hope you have a good trip home tomorrow," the RV driver offered. "And that we might be fortunate to find bears as big as your two."

"Good luck," John and I responded in unison.

Chapter 16

We stopped at the marina office, where we heard a similar version of the news. The capture was the talk of the town. We were supportive but cautious in our responses lest we inadvertently indicated we knew more than we should have. A hand drawn poster on the wall caught my attention with its request to residents to help the college girls and their parents, now in town, by providing accommodation, meals and finances. A public barbecue of support was being arranged to take place the next day in one of the city parks.

I pulled John aside and shared an idea. He agreed, so I turned to the dockmaster.

"Sir, my partner and I have more bear meat than we really need. We'd be happy to donate the meat from one of our kills for the event tomorrow. We both have daughters and are sympathetic to the victims' plight. Do you know this contact person named on the poster who seems to be organizing things?"

"That's a very generous offer gentlemen. Let me call Diane immediately. I know her well as she's the wife of my peer and competitor at one of the other marinas."

"Which marina is that?" I ask.

"The newest one - China Creek."

"We passed that on the way in here, way south of town right?" I glanced quickly at John, the lines on his face showing some concern. Mirroring mine no dount.

"Yep, you got it. Her husband's name is Jared. The three of us were in the same year at school here. Have been the best of friends ever since. Jared will be busy this time of day but I'm sure Diane will come quickly to get the meat and store it in a freezer so it keeps well. I'll send her down to your boat as soon as she arrives. Shouldn't be long as she lives close-by. Thanks again for your offer. Have a good trip home tomorrow."

Despite a twinge of wariness over a person close to the business of the previous marina coming by, we were both feeling good and chatted happily as we wheeled our bikes and their loads along the wooden docks to our boat. In a small way we were partially atoning for our sins against the two rapists. Not enough by any stretch of the imagination to offset our dastardly 'excessive force' deeds, but in the right direction. We talked about offering $100 each to the fund that was being established to cover the girls' medical expenses, another small offering that would help our consciences.

We'd undone our camping gear and the meat of one bear and loaded both bikes and a trailer onto the boat when Diane appeared with a small cart used by boat owners to transport supplies between parking lot and dock berth. She hailed us enthusiastically.

"Hi gents. Thank you so much for your kind offer. Are you really sure you want to part with your kill?"

"Absolutely," John replied. "With one condition. If the four victims are healthy enough, and brave enough, to attend tomorrow's event, they get to eat the tenderloin. We think that would be fitting."

"Couldn't agree more. Are you sure you won't be able to attend? It would be nice to recognize your generosity."

I swivel my head back and forth as a negative response, while John continues the interaction.

"Sorry, we need to be heading homeward. It's a long haul back. And even if we could attend we'd insist on being anonymous. The focus should be on the victims, no one else."

"That's a nice sentiment. I'll share it with those who ask."

"No fuss please. We both have two daughters and are very conscious of their potential vulnerability. This whole incident makes us sick. We're glad the perpetrators have been caught."

Diane lowers her head and pauses, seems to be thinking about something, finally stretches up and says, "There's more to their capture than has been made public or will ever be revealed. I shouldn't really tell you, but since you are leaving and are so supportive I'll share what I know."

She wrings her hands together and says "My husband's brother is a Mountie who's been actively engaged on the team looking for the rapists since the outset. Apparently the cops received a tip from a phone at a trailhead parking lot northeast of town indicating where the vile pair could be found in their hunting camp. Turns out some other hunters apparently had stumbled across the pair, recognized them, and had taken the law into their own hands by …"

She pauses, takes a couple of deep breaths, and continues. "… by ah, mutilating them, ah, so they can't rape anymore, if you get my meaning. The cops aren't working very hard to try and catch whoever did it, saying they expect the guys took off back to Nanaimo or wherever they drove in from, and because they have some empathy for their deed."

I manage a vociferous "Wow! Hard to believe," as I look at John, stalling while I try to think of a more appropriate response. In the end I choose not to say anything more. And John, thank heavens, rescues me.

"We appreciate your telling us Diane, and be assured we won't pass it on. Too bad more fathers of girls will never know. Something to think about, that's for sure."

Diane is clearly embarrassed and concerned at telling us. "I beg you to keep this to yourselves please. I probably shouldn't have said anything, but too late now. I'm glad the creeps got what they deserved."

She turns away, transfers the last leg of bear meat to her cart and prepares to leave. I ask her to wait a minute, telling her we also want to make a small financial donation. She looks at us quizzingly. I take $200 cash out of my wallet and pass it over. "That's in memory of our daughters. Add it to the fund."

"You two are the best," she responds. "Thanks again so much. We'll think of you tomorrow as we feast on this wonderful gift, and I'll pass the funds on to the parents. Please come back and see us again."

With that she trundles off, and John and I share a high-five and a big sigh of relief. Tomorrow's journey home has just been made a little more enjoyable with the extra news and our heart-felt donations.

And maybe indeed in a year's time, we'll feel brave enough to make a return visit. We'll just have to wait and see what transpires in the meantime.